TALL, DARK AND SEXY

The men who never fail—seduction included!

Brooding, successful and arrogant, these men have a dangerous glint in their eye and can sweep any female they desire off her feet. But now there's only one woman each man wants—and each will use their wealth, power, charm and irresistibly seductive ways to claim her!

Don't miss any of the titles in this exciting collection:

The Billionaire's Virgin Bride
Helen Brooks

His Mistress by Marriage
Lee Wilkinson

The British Billionaire Affair
Susanne James

The Millionaire's Marriage Revenge
Amanda Browning

LEE WILKINSON attended an all-girls school, where her teachers, often finding her daydreaming, declared that she "lived inside her own head," and that is still largely true today. Until her marriage, she had a variety of jobs, ranging from PA to a departmental manager, to modeling swimsuits and underwear.

As an only child and avid reader from an early age, Lee began writing when she and her husband and their two children moved to Derbyshire. She started with short stories and magazine serials before going on to write romances for Harlequin Mills & Boon.

A lover of animals, after Lee lost Kelly, her adored German shepherd, she took in a rescue dog named Thorn, who looks like a pit bull and acts like a big softy, apart from when the postman calls. Then he has to be restrained, otherwise he goes berserk and shreds the mail.

Traveling has always been one of Lee's main pleasures, and after crossing Australia and America in a motor home, and traveling round the world on two separate occasions she still, periodically, suffers from itchy feet.

She enjoys walking and cooking, log fires and red wine, music and the theater, and still much prefers books to television—both reading and writing them.

HIS MISTRESS BY MARRIAGE

LEE WILKINSON

~ TALL, DARK AND SEXY ~

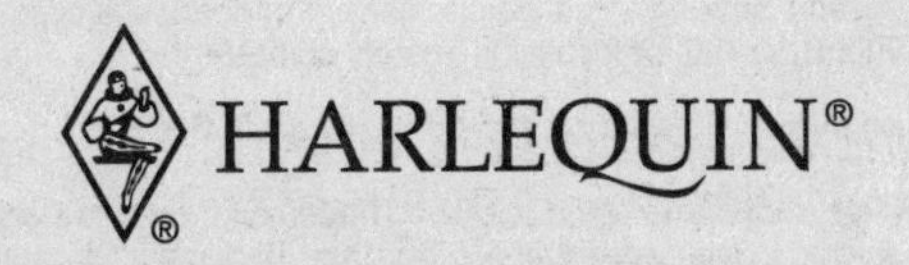

TORONTO • NEW YORK • LONDON
AMSTERDAM • PARIS • SYDNEY • HAMBURG
STOCKHOLM • ATHENS • TOKYO • MILAN • MADRID
PRAGUE • WARSAW • BUDAPEST • AUCKLAND

ISBN-13: 978-0-373-82350-5
ISBN-10: 0-373-82350-9

HIS MISTRESS BY MARRIAGE

First North American Publication 2008.

This edition published by arrangement with Harlequin Books S.A.

www.eHarlequin.com

Printed in U.S.A.

CHAPTER ONE

IT WAS twilight when they drew to a halt at the crossroads. The engine of the hired car—which Gerald had accepted on sufferance, the model he'd set his heart on being unavailable—idled sweetly.

'Which way now, darling?' he asked, in the exaggeratedly polite tone Deborah knew was meant to show his impatience.

'Straight across,' she told him. 'The village is half a mile or so further on.'

He engaged first gear and let in the clutch with unnecessary violence. His way of making it plain that he resented being forced to come.

But neither Deborah's mother, who had fallen and fractured her hip, nor her brother Paul, with business commitments and a heavily pregnant wife, would be able to get over to New York for their spring wedding.

They had always been a very close-knit and loving family—until she had broken that bond and exiled herself. But now, after being away so long, she wanted to see them, wanted them to meet her fiancé before the marriage took place.

'We can always get together some time in the future,' Gerald had said, when she'd first broached the subject. 'With only a couple of weeks to the wedding, and a weekend in LA with my parents scheduled, I won't have a spare minute…'

Gerald Justin Delcy, blonde and good-looking, head of the New York branch of the Los Angeles-based Delcy Fashion House and son of the founder, was used to having his own way both in business matters and with adoring females.

When she had been transferred from the Paris branch to New York, just under a year ago, Deborah had become one of them. Almost.

Attracted by his handsome face and his smooth sophistication, she had taken her long ash-blonde hair up into a chignon, learnt to make the most of her green eyes—eyes that changed colour with the light—and dieted until she was as slender and ethereal as he liked his women.

In fact she had done everything possible to be the kind of woman he went for.

Everything except sleep with him.

When he had finally asked her to marry him she had been delighted. It was what she had been hoping for for months.

So what had made her hesitate?

Why try to fool herself? It had been the mention of David in *World Beat* that had unsettled her.

That brief article—seen by chance.

David Westlake, a self-made multimillionaire at under thirty, has stepped in to save one of London's well-known landmarks.

When, following years of neglect, St Mary's House was declared structurally unsound and threatened with demolition, the philanthropic businessman bought the handsome Edwardian property for an undisclosed sum.

After the major rebuilding work is completed, he intends to refurbish St Mary's and give it to MHYA, a charity which has plans to turn the house into an education centre for mentally handicapped youngsters and adults.

At the beginning of last year Mr Westlake, a noted workaholic and a man of international stature in the business world, financed the building and equipping of a new special care wing at St Jude's Hospital.

It had been enough to open the floodgates to memories she'd been endeavouring to keep out.

Though David was a businessman, with no special interest in art and design, they had met at an art agent's summer party three years ago.

She had noticed him immediately. So had Claire, her friend and flatmate.

Well-dressed, his haircut smart but conventional, he hadn't fitted in with the rather arty crowd. Quite a lot of the younger people there, including herself, had been college graduates. But he was older, more mature, with a quiet air of authority and a mixture of asceticism and sensuality that had fascinated her from the start.

Judging by the way most of the woman there had done a double-take, they had felt much the same.

Claire, red-haired and blue-eyed, pretty as a picture, had made a dead set at him. But, though he had smiled and talked, he hadn't responded to her determined attempts to flirt with him.

It had been Deborah he had singled out.

Appearing by her side, he had said, 'I was starting to wonder why I'd come to this party, but now I know.' Looking into her green eyes he'd added, 'You have the most beautiful eyes I've ever seen. They're like opals.'

She had heard it said that the factors of love were hope and chance. She hadn't been hoping—her career was absorbing her thoughts at that time—but she had seen herself reflected in his dark pupils, and whatever made the world move had moved the world for her then.

Though not handsome in the film-star sense, he was one of the most attractive men she had ever seen, with the lithe, casual grace of an athlete and the charisma of a guru.

After twenty-one years of steady family affection, her life had caught fire. At that instant she had fallen in love with a depth and passion she'd thought would last her whole life through.

Not very long afterwards she had learnt that Delcy Fashion House liked her portfolio and were offering her a job in Paris that most aspiring fashion designers would have died for.

Unwilling to leave David, she had turned it down without a qualm.

After only a matter of weeks, having described himself as a one-woman man, he had asked her to marry him. Knowing herself to be a one-man woman, she had joyfully accepted.

When he'd slid a beautiful engagement ring onto her finger she had wanted Claire and the whole world to share in her happiness.

The world had appeared largely indifferent, and Claire—though flaunting a new and handsome boyfriend—had seemed strangely quiet.

David's two sisters, and her own family, had been delighted by the news.

Having had enough of living in a London flat, David had suggested they bought a house in the country, so they had started to look for their ideal home.

At first they had met with little or no success. Then, in late October, a seven-bedroomed Elizabethan manor house, with gardens, stabling, and a sixteenth-century walled garden, had come onto the market.

Rothlands, the house agent had informed them, was a two-storey place built of mellow stone, with twisted chimneys and mullioned windows. It was unusual in that the hall wasn't central, but lay about two thirds along the structure.

Both the house and the stables, he'd warned, were in need of substantial repairs.

Situated in pleasant, rolling country, about a mile from the picturesque village of Pityme, the property was within reasonable commuting distance of London.

Interested, despite the house agent's warning and the high price, they'd gone down to see it.

They had found the whole place was semi-derelict. The front door hung loose on its hinges, glass had gone from the window frames, part of the roof had fallen in, and ivy encroached everywhere. Nevertheless, Deborah had fallen in love with it at first sight.

'Like it?' David had asked, as they'd walked hand in hand through the ruined rooms.

Knowing the owner was asking far too high a price, and well aware it would need tens of thousands spending on it, she had hesitated.

'You don't need to say anything,' he'd told her with a smile. 'I only have to look at your face to know you do, and it will be a great place to bring up our children.'

Deborah had been filled with such joy and gladness she had felt incandescent.

That blazing happiness had lasted for only a few short weeks. Then David's betrayal had left her gutted and empty—a burnt-out shell at twenty-one.

Matters had been complicated by the fact that her brother Paul and Kathy, David's younger sister, had fallen in love and planned to marry in the following spring.

Her pride at stake, and unwilling, for the sake of family harmony, to let the others know what David had done, Deborah had announced that she had made a mistake and was ending the engagement.

Pressed for a reason, she had told them that her career was more important to her than marriage.

They had all been staggered, and in their various ways had tried to get her to change her mind.

Paul had been one of the most persistent.

It had been like a giant hand squeezing her heart, and finally, after swearing him to secrecy, she had told him part of the truth that David had been having an affair with Claire. That wasn't even the whole story, although it was bad enough. But she just couldn't bear to reveal to Paul the worst of David's sins.

'I'm quite sure you're wrong, sis.' He had sounded deeply upset.

'I only wish I was.'

'What does David say about it?'

'He doesn't know I know.'

'You haven't talked to him?'

'No. I couldn't bring myself to… And it wasn't necessary. Claire admitted it. She almost taunted me about it.'

'Perhaps she was just trying to cause trouble—to come between you and David?' Paul had suggested.

'Why would she try to come between David and me when she has a boyfriend of her own?'

'She might have a boyfriend of her own, but if she's always fancied David—'

'That's the whole point. She *has* always fancied him, and she's beautiful and alluring—'

'And used to men falling for her. So if David ignored her… Well, you know what they say about a woman scorned. She could have been lying,' Paul had pointed out.

'I'm convinced she wasn't. Anyway, I saw them together—saw them kissing.'

For a moment Paul had looked startled, then he'd said, 'Just a kiss doesn't prove anything.'

Unwilling to go into the painful details she'd witnessed, she'd said, 'It was more than just a kiss, believe me.'

He'd thought it over for a while, before asking seriously, 'Just how much does David mean to you?'

'Less than nothing,' she had lied, full of bitterness and anger.

'Are you sure?' Paul had persisted.

'Absolutely sure. I never want to see or hear of him again. I'll stick with my career.'

Plainly unhappy, but respecting her confidence, Paul had said nothing further.

Needing desperately to get away, she had contacted Delcy Fashion House and asked if they were still interested in employing her.

Finding they were, she had accepted their terms and fled to France.

For over two years, while she had lived in Paris and pursued her career—not even returning for Kathy and Paul's wedding—she had struggled not to think about David, to put him out of her mind, to forget about him.

Since coming to New York she had more or less succeeded. Only occasionally, in an unguarded moment, had a sense of hurt and loss struck, savage as a knife thrust.

But ever since she'd read that article about him, he had become a spectre that haunted her night and day, refusing to be banished.

During fashionable lunches and elegant dinners, in the midst of bright talk and laughter, she would fall silent, his dark face filling her mind.

In spite of all the grief and heartache he'd caused her, it had taken her a tremendous effort of will to concentrate on the glowing future that beckoned and agree to marry Gerald.

Her initial hesitation had both surprised and baffled him, but as soon as his engagement ring was on her finger, and the wedding plans made, his confidence had returned.

So much so that when she had persisted in what he saw as her unreasonable demand that Gerald should meet her family, he had said dismissively, 'You haven't lived at home since you went to college. Surely it can't be that important that you visit right now?'

But it was. So important—although she couldn't have

said exactly why—that she had threatened to postpone the wedding.

Forced into a corner by her unusual show of determination, Gerald had reluctantly agreed, and now they were on their way to stay the weekend with her mother and stepfather in Seldon.

Not without some acrimony.

Gerald had spent most of the flight complaining that he really had better things to do than visit the back of beyond.

Which she couldn't deny Seldon was.

A rural backwater where little happened, improvements and modernisation had passed Seldon by. The village street, with its cobbled gutters and picturesque cottages, had barely changed in the last two centuries—apart from the fact that it was lit with electricity now rather than gas lamps.

'Despite the fact that it's only thirty miles from London, it looks like a place where time stands still,' Gerald remarked, his voice contemptuous.

'I suppose in a way it is,' she agreed levelly. 'But Mum seems happy here.'

After her first husband had died, some five years ago, Laura Hartley had met and married Alan Dowling, a widower and the village's general practitioner.

They lived next to the church in a well-built, spacious house which had once been the vicarage. A single-storey addition built onto one side had been Alan Dowling's surgery for the past twenty years.

As they drew up outside, the door was opened by a middle-aged woman Deborah had never seen before.

'Do come in. Mrs Dowling's been waiting for you.' Then, by way of explanation, 'I'm Mrs Peele. I live just a few doors away. I've been acting as housekeeper since Mrs Dowling's been laid up.'

Gerald retrieved their cases from the boot and they followed Mrs Peele into the hall, where she took charge of their luggage before showing them through to the front parlour.

It had been turned into a temporary bedroom, and Laura Dowling was lying in bed propped up on pillows. Soft fair hair framed a gentle, young-looking face, and her eyes were the same iridescent blue-green as her daughter's.

'Darling!' She held out her arms. 'How lovely to see you… It's so long since you've been home.'

Feeling the sudden prick of tears behind her eyes, Deborah bent to carefully hug the familiar figure. 'It's lovely to see you too… And this is Gerald,' she went on proudly.

He was beautifully dressed—as always—in a pale blue shirt, with a matching pure silk scarf at the neck, an Italian silk and wool loose-knit cream sweater, and handmade shoes.

Laura greeted him with a charming smile. 'I'm so pleased to meet you.'

Taking the proffered hand, he said, with more politeness than warmth, 'It's very nice to meet you, Mrs Dowling.'

'Do sit down.'

He took a seat in an armchair, while Deborah perched on the bed.

'The Friday evening surgery is usually a busy one,' Laura went on. 'It seems everyone wants to get pills and potions before the weekend. But Alan should be joining us shortly…' Then, to her daughter, 'Now, let me see your ring.'

It was a magnificent diamond cluster that any woman would have been proud to wear.

Sounding more than a little awed, Laura said, 'That's really something.'

Turning the cluster to make it sparkle, Deborah agreed, 'Yes, isn't it? Gerald chose it.'

But sometimes she saw in its place an opal solitaire that had been quite magical…

When she and David had first discussed engagement rings he'd said firmly, 'Diamonds are too banal for you. In any case, you should have something that matches your eyes.'

'An emerald?' she had suggested.

He'd shaken his head decidedly. 'You need something more subtle than emeralds. When I was in Coober Pedy last year I saw a bluey green opal that would be absolutely perfect...'

'I must say you look marvellous!' Her mother's voice broke into Deborah's thoughts. 'But you've got very thin.'

'Slim,' Gerald corrected. 'It's fashionable.'

'How are *you*, Mum?' Deborah asked quickly.

'I'm doing fine,' Laura answered with a smile. 'Another few days and I should be properly on my feet. Though obviously I won't be going to any dances just yet.'

Then, pushing her own concerns aside, Laura asked, 'I expect you've spent the day in London? Did you see Kathy and Paul, as planned?'

'Yes, we had lunch with them.'

'At Thornton Court?'

'No, we met in town.'

Her voice overly casual, Laura enquired, 'I suppose you didn't see anything of David?'

In their letters and phone calls none of the family ever mentioned David's name, and the question came with all the shock and surprise of an ambush.

It was a moment before Deborah was able to say jerkily, 'No. Why should we have done?'

'I just wondered,' Laura said vaguely. Then, 'What did you do after lunch?'

'Paul had to go back to work, so we went round Harrods with Kathy. There were still a few baby things she needed, and she said these days Paul never has time for shopping.'

'Since your father died and Paul's been running the company he's been under a lot of pressure.'

Deborah, who had always been very close to her brother, sighed. 'I gather that to add to his problems his right-hand man has had a heart attack?'

'Yes, poor John Lattimer. Though he seems to be making good progress and is hoping to be back at work in a month or so. In the meantime Paul is working all hours God sends. But Hartley Electronics has always meant a lot to him, and now he's going to have a son of his own to leave it to, I imagine it means even more.' Laura frowned. 'I only hope he can manage to weather this latest crisis and avoid a hostile takeover. It would finish him to lose the company.'

'He mentioned that Crofts were putting on the pressure, but he seems confident he can keep them at bay,' Deborah said.

'I certainly hope so.' Laura was, and always had been, concerned about both her children.

After a pause, she changed the subject. 'I've been meaning to ask you—do you ever hear from Claire?'

Every single nerve in her body tightening, Deborah said in a carefully casual tone, with just the right amount of queary, 'Claire?'

'Claire Bolton…your college friend.'

'No. Why do you ask?'

'When I was in hospital, with my hip, her mother happened to be in the next bed. She told me that Claire had left her husband and gone to live with another man.'

'Left her husband?'

'She married Rory McInnes…'

'How long ago?' Deborah was pleased by the steadiness of her voice.

'Nearly three years, I gather. You didn't know about the wedding?'

'No…' She took a deep, painful breath. 'We lost touch when I went to work in Paris.'

Though her mother's quick glance was thoughtful, she said nothing.

'What happened to the child?' Deborah pursued, after a moment. 'Claire did have a child, didn't she?'

'Yes, a son called Sean. Apparently when she went to live with her new boyfriend she left the child with Rory. But *he* refused to take responsibility, claiming she was already pregnant when they met and the boy wasn't his...'

Deborah felt the pain in her chest expand. *She* knew whose child it was...

'Claire's elder sister, who's married and has three children of her own, is taking care of the poor little soul.'

Seeing the look on her daughter's face, Laura said anxiously, 'I hope the news hasn't upset you? I know you once thought a lot of Claire.'

'Yes, I did.' *Once.* 'But you didn't?'

'No.' Laura was nothing if not honest. 'I'm afraid I never really liked her. I always thought she was man-mad—and bitterly jealous of you.'

'Jealous of me?' Deborah asked in surprise.

'She seemed to want whatever you had.'

Deborah bit her lip.

'And though she was one of the prettiest girls I've ever seen,' Laura continued, 'and you and she were such good friends, I felt sure she had no principles. I was very pleased when Paul met Kathy and fell in love with her. At one time I was afraid he would get involved with Claire...'

Instead it had been David.

'But that's all over and done with.' Laura made a movement, as if brushing the past away. 'Now, tell me about your job. Are you happy living in New York and being chief designer for a top fashion company?'

Before she could answer, Gerald said, 'Of course she's happy. Who wouldn't be? Deborah's an extremely lucky woman.'

'And talented,' Laura observed quietly.

Looking slightly put out, Gerald agreed, 'That goes without saying. Otherwise she wouldn't be working for Delcy. As it is, she has everything she could possibly wish for—a glamorous lifestyle, a fantastic wardrobe, trips to the fashion capitals of the world… And now, after some initial hesitation, she's going to marry the boss.'

'Some hesitation?' Laura frowned.

'I don't know why I didn't accept straight away,' Deborah said quickly.

His voice dry, Gerald opined, 'A ploy to make me keener, no doubt.'

'No, it wasn't that,' she denied, but was irritatingly aware that he didn't believe her.

'It's as well to be sure,' Laura remarked quietly.

And Deborah knew without a shadow of a doubt that, despite his good looks and his wealthy background, her mother didn't like Gerald.

Any more than Paul had liked him.

Trying to stifle her keen disappointment, she told herself that when they got to know him better they might change their minds. And if they didn't it was too bad. She loved him and was sticking with the life she had chosen.

Making a determined effort, Laura pursued, 'I expect all your wedding plans are made?'

'Yes, we're—'

'Which is just as well,' Gerald broke in, his grey eyes showing his impatience. 'With having to be away this weekend we've very little time left.'

At that moment Alan Dowling appeared. He was tall and balding, with a pleasantly ugly face and an air of quiet confidence.

When the men had been introduced, and Alan had offered his congratulations and kissed Deborah, he produced bottles and glasses. 'This calls for a celebration. What will you have?'

Over drinks they talked—Laura and Alan with forced cheerfulness, Gerald with more than a touch of condescension.

Listening to them, Deborah sighed inwardly. The fact that her mother and stepfather were having to try so hard only emphasised the yawning gap between them and her future husband.

She could only hope that next weekend's trip to Los Angeles to meet Gerald's parents would be a great deal easier.

'Well, of course New York is *the* place to be,' her fiancé was saying. 'I can't imagine anyone wanting to live anywhere else.'

'It's perhaps as well *someone* does,' Alan observed quizzically. 'Otherwise it would be even more noisy and crowded than it is.'

His manner more than a touch condescending, Gerald asked, 'Have you ever been?'

'When I was a young man I was offered a post in one of New York's teaching hospitals. But after a year I gave it up and returned home. Though the Big Apple's a great place in a lot of ways, I wouldn't want to live there permanently.'

'You'd sooner be a GP in Seldon?' Gerald queried, in a tone of absolute disbelief.

His voice mild, Alan answered, 'As a matter of fact, I would.'

'I'd have thought that anyone with an ounce of intelligence would be bored to tears.'

Alan shrugged. 'Seldon wouldn't be everyone's cup of tea, but it takes all sorts to make a world.'

'As far as I'm concerned anyone who chooses to live in a dump like this needs their head testing—'

'Did I tell you we're going to Hawaii for our honeymoon...?' Wishing unhappily that she hadn't insisted on coming home, Deborah rushed headlong into the conversation in an attempt to divert attention away from Gerald's rudeness.

When Mrs Peele announced that dinner was ready it came as a relief.

The relief was short-lived.

Laura had hers on a tray, while the other three ate in the dining room. It proved to be an uncomfortable meal. Alan and Deborah tried hard to keep some kind of conversation going, but without Laura's gallant help, and in the face of Gerald's indifference, it quickly faltered and died.

After the meal, Deborah and her mother and stepfather did their best, but Gerald looked bored to tears, and, giving up the struggle to find some common ground, they went to bed at ten-thirty.

Gerald said a sullen, 'Goodnight,' and to show he was blaming her left Deborah without even a kiss.

Once in her own room, she groaned. The weekend showed every sign of being a total disaster. She couldn't wait for it to be over so they could go back to Manhattan.

On the following Sunday night, after their return flight from LA where they'd spent the weekend with Gerald's parents, Gerald insisted on stopping for a leisurely dinner at Dylan's—he refused to eat airline food—and it was quite late by the time his red, low-slung sports car drew to a halt in front of the brownstone where Deborah lived.

The past week had proved to be even more hectic than they had expected as, with a last-minute surge of activity, they had launched Delcy's summer fashion show on Fifth Avenue.

As soon as that was over, they had set off to fly to the West Coast.

Deborah had wondered a little anxiously if Gerald's parents would think she was good enough for their only son. But, seeming genuinely pleased that at thirty-two he was finally settling down to marriage, they had been charming to her, and the weekend had proved to be a great success.

Cutting the engine, Gerald jumped out and came round to open her door. As he reached into the back to retrieve her weekend case she looked along the busy street she had lived in since coming to the States.

Bright and bustling in the day, it was romantic at night, sketched in indigo and gold, with lighted windows, deep shadows, and street lamps illuminating the budding trees.

Deborah had enjoyed living on the second floor of the old brownstone, but after the wedding she would be moving into Gerald's up-market Park Avenue suite.

It was a thrilling thought.

But she would miss her flatmate Fran, not to mention Thomas, their marmalade cat, who, as a hungry stray, had made use of the fire escape and a partly open window to move in with them.

'I don't know why you put up with that flea-ridden thing,' Gerald had once said.

'He's nothing of the kind,' she had denied indignantly. 'And I like animals.'

'Well, I just hope you're not thinking of bringing him with you?'

'No. Fran's going to take care of him.'

Her fiancé had looked immeasurably relieved.

Now, as they climbed the steps, Thomas appeared from nowhere. A gregarious cat, loudly vocal in his pleasure at having her back, he wound sinuously round their ankles, nearly tripping Gerald up.

Cursing under his breath, he used a none-too-gentle foot to push the animal away.

Frowning, Deborah stooped, and, picking Thomas up, tucked him safely under her arm.

When they reached her door, Gerald asked, 'Can I come in for a coffee?'

Shaking her head, she said a little shortly, 'Better not. It's much too late.'

For one thing, after such a frenetic week, and two successive weekends of travelling, she was desperately tired. But, as Gerald had no sympathy with anyone who flagged, she hesitated to say so.

'I've hardly seen anything of you,' he complained.

'How can you say that? I've scarcely been out of your sight since Friday.'

'But I've never had you to myself.'

'All the same, it's been most enjoyable.'

Cheering up, he agreed, 'You fitted in well. Both my parents liked you.'

'I'm glad.'

Dropping her case, he said, 'If you'd put that animal down, I'd like to kiss you.'

She set Thomas on his feet, and as soon as she'd opened the door he disappeared inside, tail erect.

Gerald drew her into his arms and began to kiss her with unrestrained eagerness.

Most of the women he'd fancied had sooner or later succumbed to his charm and ended up in bed with him. Others had actively made the running.

But Deborah had done neither.

Though she had clearly been attracted to him, with a cool self-restraint that had first annoyed and then intrigued him, she had kept him at arm's length, kept him interested.

He had proposed, confident that with a ring on her finger she would loosen up.

She hadn't.

Discreetly, he had used other women to meet his needs, but it was *her* he wanted. And now he could hardly wait for their wedding night.

After a while, Deborah broke the kiss and drew away. 'I'd better go. We both have to be up early tomorrow. Thank you for a lovely weekend.'

Finding he still looked disposed to linger, she blew him a kiss, picked up her case, and slipped inside, closing the door behind her.

A table-lamp cast a pool of light in the far corner, leaving the rest of the room in deep shadow. The curtains were pulled too, which indicated that, rather than being out, Fran had gone to bed.

Knowing that any streak of brightness beneath her bedroom door sometimes disturbed her flatmate, Deborah set her case and bag down and bolted the door without putting on the main lights, while she listened to Gerald's retreating footsteps.

When she turned, it was to find a tall, powerfully built man just rising from one of the armchairs. The shock brought a gasp to her lips and made her heart start to race unevenly.

Then common sense reasserted itself, and she realised he must be Fran's latest boyfriend. But why had he been sitting there in the semi-darkness if Fran was in bed?

Struggling to hide her momentary panic, she began, 'You must be—' then stopped dead.

He was standing in the shadows, and she couldn't see his face properly, but his height and build and the set of that dark head were burnt into her brain.

David!

No, it couldn't possibly be. She was just letting a passing similarity throw her.

After she had given him back his ring and run, how many times had a glimpse of a broad-shouldered man with thick dark hair stopped her breath and set her heart pounding?

How many times, sick and shaken, had she realised that the likeness was mostly in her own mind?

Taking an involuntary step backwards, she bumped into her case as she fumbled for the switch and flooded the room with light.

But this time it *was* David.

CHAPTER TWO

FOR A moment or two, feeling as if she had been kicked in the solar plexus, she simply stared at him.

He had a strong face, with a straight nose, level brows, a beautiful mouth, and a cleft in his squarish chin. His handsome, thickly-lashed eyes were cornflower-blue, and the crisp dark hair that tried to curl was as vital as the man himself.

'What are *you* doing here?' she whispered.

'Waiting for you...'

His gaze moved with slow deliberation over her gleaming ash-blonde hair, her heart-shaped face, her slender figure in the mulberry-coloured silk suit, and her slim ankles and feet shod in matching suede court shoes.

'But I gather from your flatmate that you've been away for the weekend.' He made it sound as though she had no right to be away.

'Why are you here? What do you want?' Her throat was dry and her voice sounded hoarse, impeded.

'I've come to escort you back to London.'

The curt announcement shook her rigid.

Sucking in breath, she said, 'I don't need escorting back to London. This is where I live.'

'I'm aware of that.'

'And I'm due to be married in a week's time—'

'I'm aware of that too. But you may have to postpone the wedding.'

'I shall do no such thing!' Deborah gasped.

'You'll do whatever's necessary,' he bit out.

'What makes you think you can force your way in here and start dishing out orders?' she demanded.

'I didn't force my way in. Your flatmate, who expected you back ages ago, let me in and allowed me to wait.' Glancing at his watch, he added grimly, 'I've been waiting over five hours.'

'Really? You must think it's important.'

A white line appeared around his mouth. 'I do. And so does your mother and the rest of the family. But obviously you don't.'

Scared by his quiet fury, she began unsteadily, 'As I haven't the least idea what you're talking about—'

'I'm talking about Paul.'

'What about Paul?' Deborah asked quickly.

'As you know, he's in hospital, and—'

Horrified, she cried, 'Paul's in hospital? But I *didn't* know.'

'Don't give me that.' His eyes were hard. 'You just don't care.'

'I swear I didn't know!'

'It's no use lying. When your mother couldn't get hold of you she appealed to me for help. I phoned Delcy Fashion House myself.'

'Gerald and I flew to LA on Friday evening.'

'This was Friday morning.'

'I was out. We had a fashion show.'

'So I was told. When they were unable to contact you, I insisted on speaking to Delcy. I made it clear you were needed in London without delay. He promised to tell you as soon as you got back.'

'Gerald knew!'

'Yes, he knew.'

Blankly, she said, 'He didn't tell me.'

Seeing the look of disgust on David's face, she tried to

excuse her fiancé. 'He had so much to do...perhaps it slipped his mind.'

'You mean it might have been inconvenient for him.'

With their weekend schedule in place, it *would* have been, as far as Gerald was concerned.

Biting her lip, she asked, 'Why is Paul in hospital? What's wrong?'

'He's been injured in a car accident.'

Her green eyes fixed on his face, she whispered, 'How did it happen? How bad is it?'

But she already knew the answer to her last question. If it hadn't been serious David would never have come all this way.

Flatly, he said, 'He was taking a corner when his car swerved off the road and rolled down an embankment. After he was cut free from the wreckage he was taken to St Jude's with multiple injuries. He's on the critical list.'

Deborah blinked as the shock hit her, blurring her vision and bringing a sudden wave of giddiness and nausea. She was conscious of David's arm going round her, drawing her close, supporting her.

Then she was being guided to a chair, and her head pressed down to her knees. After a moment or so the dizziness began to pass and she struggled to sit up.

Her throat desert-dry, she said, almost pleadingly, 'But you didn't tell Gerald how bad it was?'

Even as she spoke she knew she was wrong. David would have laid it on the line. His quiet, 'I told him,' only served to confirm it.

Huskily, she queried, 'When did the accident happen?'

'Early Thursday evening. Paul was on his way home from the office...'

Thursday evening... And now it was Sunday.

'The shock caused Kathy to go into premature labour. If your mother hadn't been laid up I'm sure she would have coped, but as it is the family need your support. That's why I dropped everything and came,' he ended tonelessly.

Seeing his face, the judgement and censure there, made her say sharply, 'You didn't *have* to come. I could have made the journey without your help.'

'I wasn't sure you would.'

Deborah was so shocked she could hardly respond to his words. 'What do mean, you weren't sure I would?'

'When we didn't hear from you, I presumed that either you didn't want to come or Delcy had managed to talk you out of it.'

She jumped to her feet and faced him, her hands balled into fists. 'What right had you to presume a thing like that?'

He gave her a look that was a challenge. 'In the circumstances, isn't it as well I did?'

Of course he was right. After Gerald's failure to tell her she could find no defence.

'I would have come at once if only I'd known,' she informed him tightly.

'You think Delcy would have let you?'

'He couldn't have stopped me.'

'I beg leave to doubt that. He has some pretty powerful weapons.'

Her eyes sparkling with anger, she demanded, 'What do you mean?'

'Well, I know how important your *career* is to you.'

'You think it's more important to me than my *family*?'

'It was more important to you than *me*.'

She felt as though she'd been struck. But after all she'd said there was no way she could deny it.

'And no doubt the chance to be Mrs Gerald Delcy must count for a lot.'

It *had* done.

Now suddenly it counted for nothing.

What *did* count was her family. Her mother and Kathy,

and her brother, who might be dying. Who might already be dead.

She bit her lip until she tasted blood. 'I'll ring the hospital.'

'I had a word with them just before you got back. Paul's condition is virtually unchanged. It's still touch and go.'

She swallowed hard. 'Is there any news of Kathy?'

'She had a baby boy in the early hours of Friday morning. It wasn't an easy birth, so they're keeping her in hospital until Monday.'

'How is she coping?'

'Very well, considering. But she's chaffing because she can't be with Paul. He's drifting in and out of consciousness, and the doctor says it might prevent him sinking into a coma if someone could sit and talk to him. As Laura's barely on her feet, both women were pinning their hopes on you,' he added.

Fiercely, Deborah blinked away the tears. She wouldn't give him the satisfaction of seeing her cry.

When she was sure she had her voice under control, she said, 'I'll phone the airport and see how soon we can get a flight.'

'There's no need,' he told her shortly. 'My private jet is waiting. Now while you let your flatmate know what's happening and pack a few things—I'm sure you'll get by without a full designer wardrobe—I'll arrange for a taxi.'

Hating his sarcasm, but too fraught to fight back, she picked up her weekend case and bag.

'Don't forget your passport,' he called after her as she hurried into her bedroom, her eyes gritty with unshed tears.

It was obvious from the way he was treating her that he held her as well as Gerald in contempt.

She was barely inside her room when there was a knock. Fran, clad in her mules and night things, slipped in and closed the door behind her.

Lowering her voice, she said hurriedly, 'I'm sorry if you would have preferred me not to let him wait. But when he rang the bell I was trying to stop Thomas playing Kill the Hedgehog with my best hairbrush, and I wasn't quite focused. After I told him you were away for the weekend he introduced himself and explained that he was here on an urgent family matter. Then, when I opened the door, he simply walked in. He wanted to know how long you'd be. I told him roughly when I was expecting you, and he informed me very politely that he'd wait. Though he's extremely dishy, he's also quite formidable, and I didn't have the courage to ask him to leave. I hope you don't mind?'

Deborah, who had been opening drawers to find undies and nightwear, said, 'Of course I don't mind. My brother's been involved in an accident and—'

'Yes, I know. I couldn't help but overhear. I'm so sorry. Is there anything I can do?'

'Will you look in the cupboard for a bigger case? Oh, and a handbag. This one's a bit small.'

As Deborah took suits and dresses from the wardrobe, Fran threw a case on the bed and unzipped it. 'Is that OK?'

'Fine.'

'And a handbag…anything else?'

'Perhaps you'll be kind enough to phone Gerald?' Deborah asked.

'Don't you want to talk to him yourself?'

'No,' Deborah said shortly. She didn't trust herself to speak to him until she knew that Paul was out of danger. 'Tomorrow morning will do,' she added. 'Then you can tell him everything that's happened and what's been said.'

Fran, who was no fool, asked carefully, 'You mean an edited version?'

Bundling her belongings into the case anyhow, Deborah shook her head. 'No, I mean *exactly* what's been said.'

'Sure?'

'Sure.' After what he'd done, she had no intention of trying to spare his feelings.

'OK, that's fine by me.' Fran, though always perfectly civil to Gerald, had never tried to hide the fact that she didn't like him.

While Deborah finished packing, swapped her things from one handbag to another and found her passport, she asked Fran, 'How did you get on with…David?' She found it difficult to say his name.

'At first I tried to be sociable and talk. He answered courteously enough, but that was all—if you see what I mean?'

Yes, Deborah could easily see how, in the grim mood he was in, he would have frozen off Fran's polite attempts at conversation.

'When I finally gave up he just sat glowering into space, looking blacker and blacker as the time dragged on. I thought he was simply in a foul temper, but I see now that he must have been worried. As he clearly didn't want my company, an early night seemed indicated, so I made him a sandwich and a pot of coffee and went to bed.'

'I'm sorry if it's spoilt your Sunday evening.'

'No, it hasn't. I finally got round to reading *Scarlet and Gold*.'

'Well, thanks for coping.'

'No problem… I only hope things aren't as bad as they sound, so you'll be able to go ahead with the wedding as planned.'

Fran's comment about the wedding brought Deborah up short. Her mind was in turmoil.

Did she want to go ahead with the wedding?

Gerald's failure to tell her about Paul had certainly damaged their relationship, though she wasn't yet sure if it was completely beyond repair. She would need to think the whole thing over very carefully, and she couldn't possibly do that right now.

Giving Fran a quick hug, she promised, 'I'll keep in touch and let you know what's happening.'

Then, having zipped up her case and collected her bag, she hurried through to the living room, where David was stooping to rub behind Thomas's ear.

He straightened, and, relieving her of her case, said, 'The taxi should be here any minute.'

Thomas looked up and miaowed at her.

As she bent to stroke him David said shortly, 'If you're quite ready, we'd better get a move on.'

Nettled by his curtness, the way he was venting his anger and impatience on her, she lifted her chin and led the way down the stairs.

As they descended the front stoop their taxi drew up with a rush. Tossing her case in the back, David said, 'JFK, please—as fast as you can.'

The moment they were settled their driver pulled out and, dodging between the late-night traffic streams with a fine disregard for life and limb, headed for Queens.

As they sped through a set of lights and swung round a corner, Deborah was thrown against her companion. Hastily moving away, she glanced at him. From his air of unruffled calm, she judged that he was no stranger to New York driving.

Noting her look, he asked sardonically, 'Not too fast for you, I trust?'

'It can't be fast enough for me,' she responded tightly.

Only too aware that Paul was lying battling for his life, might have already lost the battle, she clenched her teeth until her jaw ached.

If only she'd known earlier she would have already been by his side, giving him what help she could, and it just might have made a difference.

One thing she was absolutely sure of: if he didn't pull through she would never forgive Gerald.

But he *would* pull through. Paul was a fighter, and he had a lot to live for.

In spite of that attempt to reassure herself she felt a sudden sense of despair, and was unable to hold back the tears.

David turned towards her, and, touching her wet cheek with a single fingertip, said mockingly, 'You don't need to put on a show of grief for me. Unless, of course, it happens to be genuine.'

For a second she stared at him blankly, then, with anger sending adrenaline pumping into her bloodstream, she cried passionately, 'How can you be so utterly heartless? I *care* about Paul.'

'I must admit if that near faint was acting it was pretty good. You almost had me convinced.'

'Almost!' Her eyes flashed. 'Do you think I pretended to faint just so you'd think better of me?'

'Well, it might have stemmed from guilt.'

He gave her a mocking glance from beneath thick dark lashes. 'On the other hand, you might have just felt the urge to be held in my arms.'

'Of all the arrogant, conceited…'

'Detestable?' he suggested.

Taking a deep breath, she turned away and stared resolutely through the window. She wouldn't give him the satisfaction of crossing swords with him.

When they reached the airport it was relatively quiet. Brisk and businesslike now, David took them through the formalities before suggesting, 'As it will be ten minutes or so before we can board, perhaps you'd like a coffee?'

Still smarting from his whiplash tongue, she would have dearly loved to say a dismissive, No, thanks. But she was longing for a drink and couldn't bring herself to refuse.

The coffee arrived quickly. It was hot and strong and reviving.

As she sipped, she found her glance drawn to his half-averted face—the face she had thought never to see again, the face she had once loved more than life itself. His strong profile still had the power to twist her heartstrings, and his air of aloofness made her want to cry.

But she wouldn't let him affect her. Any feeling she had had for him was in the past. All that remained was bitterness and disillusionment.

Deliberately she switched her thoughts back to Paul. Knowing that if… No, not if—*when* he recovered, after his wife and child one of his first thoughts would be for the company, she asked, 'Do you happen to know who's in charge at Hartleys?'

David turned his head, and his dark blue eyes looked straight into hers with such anger in their depths that she all but flinched.

'Your brother might be dying, but all you care about is the company.'

Staggered by the attack, she stammered, 'I—I was just thinking that with John Lattimer off sick, and Crofts out for a takeover, there might be some serious problems.'

David laughed harshly. 'Well, I suppose you have to get your priorities right. Your career and your brother's company are obviously much more important to you than people.'

'It's not like that at all,' she protested. 'But the company means a lot to Paul…' Unable to go on, she turned away, struggling to hold back the tears.

David took her chin and turned her face back to his. Seeing the suspicious brightness of her eyes, he said cynically, 'More tears to convince me you care?'

Unable to bear his touch, she jerked her chin free and accused through stiff lips, 'You really hate me, don't you?'

'Of course I don't hate you.' Smiling ironically, he went on, 'I just don't care for the kind of woman you've become.'

'You think I'm cold and hard and uncaring.'

'And aren't you?'

'No, I'm not,' she denied unsteadily, adding in helpless anger, 'If you think so badly of me, why did you come all this way to fetch me?'

'Because your mother begged me to. And because while I was at the hospital, during a spell of consciousness, Paul asked for you.'

All the colour drained from her face. She felt chilled through and through, horrified at the thought of all the time that had elapsed since Paul had asked for her.

But why had he asked for *her* rather than Kathy?

Or had David only said that to hurt her?

No, he must be telling the truth.

Though it plainly hadn't been the truth when he'd said he didn't hate her.

Picking up her case, he asked, 'Ready to go?'

She rose to her feet unsteadily.

He put his free hand beneath her elbow, as if he doubted her ability to stand unaided.

'Please don't touch me. I can manage.'

'As you will,' he said icily, and removed his hand.

How could two people who had once purported to love each other have come to this? she wondered miserably as she followed him outside and across the tarmac, with shivers running through her that had little to do with the cool night air.

They boarded the plane in silence, and as soon as Deborah was seated, her seatbelt buckled, David brusquely excused himself and disappeared into the cockpit.

By the time he returned they were airborne.

'Luckily there's a strong tail wind,' he told her with chilling politeness, 'which should help to make it a good fast flight.'

Thank heaven for that, she thought.

'Would you care for anything to eat before we settle down?'

'No, thank you.'

'Then as there's a bedroom at the rear, with a comfortable bed, I suggest you get some sleep.'

'I couldn't.' Her voice was wobbly.

Though she felt exhausted, how could she sleep when Paul might be dying? It would be impossible.

But around David's handsome eyes and firm mouth there were unmistakable signs of weariness, and she found herself saying, 'Why don't you?'

'I'll take one of the chairs in here. Unless you're offering to share the bed?'

'No, I'm not!' she exclaimed.

'Pity. Because if you really can't sleep…'

So he didn't believe she cared enough about Paul to spend a sleepless night.

'…I could fill in for Delcy.'

Abruptly, he laughed. 'You should see your face! You look all ready to cry, "How dare you?"'

Hating his mockery, she stared at him stonily.

'What's the problem? You've slept with me before, and you seemed to enjoy it. Though I may not be as good in bed as Delcy, I remember how you used to gasp and moan when I—'

All at once his deliberate unkindness was too much to bear. Lifting her hand, she smacked his face. A stinging slap that made her palm tingle and left a white handprint that after a second or two turned a dull red.

Touching his cheek gingerly, he said, 'Well, well, well… At one time you wouldn't have said boo to a goose, let alone hit back. You've certainly changed.'

She wanted to say, *I'm what you've made me*, but it would be too revealing.

Almost admiringly, he added, 'I must say you pack a pretty fair wallop.'

'If you're expecting me to apologise—'

He shook his head. 'I'll collect on the apology in my own good time.' Picking up her case, he added, 'Now, if you insist on sleeping alone, let me show you where the bed is.'

Giving her no chance to argue, he led the way to the rear of the plane, where there was a small but luxurious bedroom.

A three-quarter bed, its duvet turned back ready, occupied most of the space. The window blinds had been pulled down and a single lamp on the bedside table cast a golden glow.

Setting her case on a rack, he enquired with a mocking smile, 'Would you like me to tuck you in?'

'No, I wouldn't,' she refused frostily, putting her handbag on the bed.

'In that case I'll say good night.'

Before she could guess his intention, he bent his head and kissed her on the lips. It was a light, arrogant kiss that held a touch of contempt.

She jerked away, and in a reflex action was lifting her hand to her lips when he caught her wrist. 'No, you don't. Once is quite enough.'

'I wasn't—' she began.

But, using the wrist he was holding, he pulled her into his arms and kissed her again. This time it was a punitive kiss that forced her head back, took her breath away, and turned her knees to water.

The emotions he engendered were so overwhelming that she thought she might faint. Then suddenly she was free, and he was closing the door behind him.

Shaking like a leaf, she sank down on the bed. How could he treat her with such casual insolence?

But he could—and had.

He was hateful! It was just as well that she'd discovered what he was really like and run away…

Angry thoughts buzzing through her mind like a swarm of bees, she took off her clothes and found a nightdress. Then, having cleaned her teeth and brushed her hair in the well-equipped *en suite* bathroom, she climbed into bed and reached to switch out the light.

She was still fuming as, with the suddenness of a mountain mist descending, sleep engulfed her.

When she awoke for a few seconds she was totally disorientated, with no idea of where she was or what she was doing there. Then it all came rushing back.

Paul's accident… Gerald's culpability in not telling her about it… David's hatred… The cruel way he had treated her…

Or had he been cruel to be kind? With a sudden disturbing clarity she recalled him once saying that anger was a more positive emotion than fear or anxiety. Had he treated her like that to make her angry? To take her mind off Paul so she could sleep?

If he had, the strategy had been successful. She had certainly slept—though at that precise moment she had no idea for how long.

Switching on the light, she peered at her watch. Still set on New York time, it said seven a.m.—which made it about lunchtime in England.

Intending to phone the hospital, she reached for her bag and felt for her mobile. It wasn't there. Changing bags in a hurry, she must have forgotten to pick it up.

Oh, please God, let Paul be all right. Don't let him be dead. Let me get there in time…

At that instant there was a tap at the door.

Without pausing to think, she called, 'Come in,' then held her breath.

But it was a white-coated steward who entered, carrying a tray of coffee.

Setting it down on the bedside table, he said, 'Good morning, Miss Hartley. Mr Westlake asked me to say that lunch will be served in fifteen minutes.'

'Thank you. How far are we from London?'

'About an hour's flying time, miss.' He went out, closing the door quietly behind him.

She swallowed two cups of the excellent coffee, then hurried through to the bathroom to shower.

When she had found clean undies, and put on a fine wool dress the colour of an aubergine, she brushed and recoiled her ash-blonde hair before making her way back to the lounge.

Dressed in grey trousers and a black polo-necked sweater, his hair neatly brushed, David was sitting at a small desk using a laptop.

Glancing up at her approach, he said without warmth, 'Good morning. How did you sleep?'

She hesitated. If she admitted that she'd slept well he would think her heartless, but she wasn't prepared to lie. 'Much better than I'd expected. Is there any news of Paul?'

'I rang the hospital a short while ago. It seems he's still holding his own.'

'Thank God,' she breathed.

After a perfunctory tap, the steward wheeled in a luncheon trolley and, after stationing it by the window, pulled up two chairs.

'I really don't think I can eat anything,' Deborah said, when David had seated her and taken his own place opposite.

He would have none of it. Filling both plates with roast chicken and salad, he said, 'Nonsense. You're far too thin as it is. And if you're going to sit with Paul you'll need to keep your strength up.'

His blue eyes pinning her, he waited until she reluctantly picked up her knife and fork before starting to eat his own meal.

They ate in silence—David as if his thoughts were elsewhere, Deborah mechanically, without tasting a thing. By the time the meal was finished they were losing height to come in to land.

In New York the weather had been dry and bright; in London it was damp and overcast as, airport formalities over, David hurried them out to his silver Jaguar.

His expression grim, he drove without speaking to St Jude's. When they reached the hospital, an efficient-looking woman at the main reception desk greeted David by name. 'Mr Westlake…it's good to have you back. Would you like to go straight up?'

They took the lift up to the second floor, and as they emerged into the echoing quietness of the special care wing a youngish, fair-haired doctor came hurrying to meet them, a frown on his face.

The two men shook hands, then David said, 'Deborah, this is Dr Hezelden… Doctor, this is Miss Hartley—Paul Hartley's sister.'

'How is he?' she asked quickly.

'The news isn't good, I'm afraid.'

All the colour drained from her face and, vaguely aware that David had put a steadying arm around her, she whispered, 'Is he dead?'

'No, no, he isn't dead. But earlier today he slipped into a coma.'

The news was bad enough, but anything that allowed some room for hope was better than the stark finality of death.

'I'm sorry if I alarmed you unduly,' Dr Hezelden apologised, looking harassed.

'That's all right.' She managed the ghost of a smile. 'May I see him?'

'Of course.'

David's arm dropped to his side and she followed the doctor as he led the way down a corridor and into a private room.

The window blind was half down, and the combination of dim light and pale green walls gave the impression of being underwater. The only sounds were a faint humming and a regular high-pitched bleep.

Looking like a ghost of the man she had lunched with only the previous week, Paul was lying on a high, narrow bed.

Tubes were taped to his arms and he was wired to a machine whose electrical impulses were monitoring his heartbeat and breathing.

While the doctor and David remained just inside the door, conversing in an undertone, Deborah went to stand by the bed.

Her brother was a nice-looking man, with unruly fair hair, good features, and his father's blue eyes. Now his eyes were closed, and cuts and bruises disfigured his ashen face. Across his chest and shoulders strapping was visible.

Choking back a sob, she turned to ask the doctor, 'Is there any chance of him hearing me?'

'I don't hold out much hope. But if you *can* get through to him it might be a big help.'

'What's your longer-term prognosis?' David queried.

'In my opinion, if he regains consciousness and can hold his own for the next seventy-two hours he stands a pretty good chance.'

'You mean he'll be out of danger?' Deborah asked.

'He should be,' the doctor said cautiously. 'Now, if you'll excuse me, I'd better get on. A nurse will be making regular checks, every twenty minutes or so, but if you have a problem or need anything just touch the red button.'

Turning to David, he added, 'By the way, the suite you asked about has become vacant. So if you'd like to make the necessary arrangements…?'

'Thanks, I will.'

The doctor hurried out and David moved to stand by the window.

Putting her jacket and bag on the sill, Deborah drew a chair up to the bedside. Taking one of Paul's hands, she held it in both of hers. It felt cold and lifeless.

'Paul?' she whispered. 'It's Deborah… I've come to see you…to be with you…'

While she talked, trying desperately to get some response, she gently chafed the hand she was holding.

She had almost given up hope when the lean fingers tightened a fraction on hers.

Slight as it was, David saw the movement and said softly, jubilantly, 'You've done it! You've got through to him.'

Suddenly realising how much David cared about Paul, she gave him a small, wavering smile.

His answering smile set her heart racing and made butterflies dance in her stomach.

After more than three years spent apart, how could he still have such a devastating effect on her? she wondered dazedly.

CHAPTER THREE

'NOW, I've some arrangements to make,' David said. 'If you don't mind staying with Paul, I need to go out for an hour or so.'

'Of course I don't mind,' she answered, without the slightest hesitation. 'It's what I came for.'

He nodded approvingly. 'In that case I'll leave you to it. I'm not sure how long it'll take, but I'll be as quick as I can.'

Reaching out a hand, he touched her cheek in the briefest of caresses, but it was enough to make her heart lurch and her breathing grow uneven.

As the door closed quietly behind him she turned back to the man held in a kind of limbo between life and death, and once again she began talking quietly to him. Telling him first that he was going to be all right, then the good news about his baby son, then anything and everything that came into her head.

She was reminiscing about their childhood, and the pets they'd had, when a young nurse came in with a tray of tea and sandwiches.

'Oh, I understood Mr Westlake was here.' She sounded disappointed.

'He had something urgent to do,' Deborah explained. 'Some arrangements to make.'

Putting the tray on a nearby trolley, the nurse said, 'Please help yourself to some tea.' Then, her voice confiding, 'I really don't know how Mr Westlake's managed to cope. Apart from an hour or so on Friday and Saturday morning, when he needed to go into the office, he's sat with Mr Hartley ever since he was admitted.'

No wonder David looked tired, Deborah thought with sudden compassion. Then, with more than a trace of bitterness, if only he'd been as trustworthy a lover as he was a friend…

'And as well as being a really nice person,' the nurse was going on, 'unlike some rich men, he does a lot of good with his money. I suppose you know he financed this entire wing?'

'Yes, I read about it.'

'All the staff think he's wonderful…'

From her sigh, it was obvious that she did too.

Then, collecting herself, the nurse set about checking on her patient before giving her verdict. 'I'm pleased to say his colour's better, and there's been a small but significant improvement in his overall condition. Now, I'm off duty until tomorrow. Alison, who'll be taking my place, is already here. She'll be popping in every twenty minutes or so. Don't let your tea get cold.' With a smile she departed.

It was early evening before David returned. By that time, after only a few hours' sleep the previous night and so much stress and tension, Deborah was starting to feel light-headed with sheer weariness.

Appearing by her elbow, he said, 'Sorry I've been so long.'

'That's all right.'

'I understand there's been some improvement?'

'Yes. He hasn't shown any further sign of awareness, but his colour's better, and the nurse seems satisfied.'

'That's great. Now, before I take you home—'

'I've no intention of going anywhere. I came to sit with Paul and—'

'You can come in again tomorrow, if that's what you

want, but at the moment you're not needed, and you're looking shattered.'

'I'm not leaving him alone.' Though she knew it was stupid, she couldn't help but feel that just by *being* there she might stop Paul slipping away.

'He won't be alone.'

'You weren't thinking of staying?'

'I'm not needed either.'

'So who will be sitting with him?'

'Look, you've made the point that you're concerned,' David said caustically. 'There's no need to overdo it.'

She flushed a dull, angry red. How could she ever have loved this man? she asked herself bitterly. He was hard and cynical and hateful…

At that moment a nurse came in and announced cheerfully, 'This time it's a full-scale check, so if you wouldn't mind giving me a few minutes…?'

'As a matter of fact we're just going.'

'I'm not leaving until you've told me who's sitting with Paul,' Deborah said in a low voice.

'Come with me and I'll show you.' Gathering up her jacket and bag, he led her to a door on the far side of the room.

Just as they reached it, it opened, and Deborah found herself face to face with her mother.

'Mum…' she said blankly.

'If you could give me a minute or so, Mrs Dowling?' the nurse called.

'Of course.'

Moving carefully, with the aid of a walking frame, Laura led the way back into a small but comfortable-looking lounge where, setting the frame aside, she hugged her daughter.

'I'm so glad you've come.'

'I can't tell you how sorry I am that I wasn't here sooner. I don't know what you must think of me...'

Overwrought, Deborah, a girl who throughout her life had rarely cried, burst into tears.

'It's all right...it's all right,' Laura soothed. 'David's explained, and we do understand. Now, don't go upsetting yourself. Everything's going to be fine.'

She padded her daughter gently on the back. 'Now you *are* here,' her mother went on after a moment, 'how long can you stay?'

Taking a deep breath, Deborah fumbled in her bag for a paper hankie. She dried her cheeks and blew her nose before answering unsteadily, 'Just as long as I'm needed.'

'What about your wedding?'

'I'm not sure...' Starting to say she hadn't decided if she was still going ahead with it, Deborah saw David's cynical expression and changed her mind. 'I'll postpone it if necessary.' Then, quickly, 'But how on earth did *you* get here? Did David bring you?'

'No. I've just come by private ambulance—with Kathy and the babe. This suite is exactly what we need, and David's arranged everything, bless him.' Laura smiled at him. 'I don't know what we would have done without him. He's been at the hospital more or less round the clock, and kept Kathy and me in the picture as well as taking over the reins at Hartleys.'

Deborah stiffened. So he was running the company! For some reason, rather than reassuring her, the knowledge that they were relying so heavily on him rattled her.

Sensing her daughter's reaction, Laura added seriously, 'He's the only man capable of doing the job and keeping the company out of trouble while Paul is laid up.'

Looking at David, meeting those deep blue eyes with spirit, Deborah asked, 'In whose opinion?'

'In Kathy's and mine,' Laura answered, with a quiet authority that surprised Deborah. Her usually gentle mother, though quite able, was rarely willing to stand up to anyone.

'He knows electronics inside out. When he took over Apex Jarvis—a company that designs and markets special electronic equipment—it was practically bankrupt. With him at the helm it's starting to make a profit.'

Then why wasn't he there, keeping up the good work? Deborah wondered, irritated by her mother's praise.

Aloud she said, 'When I asked him who was in charge at Hartleys he didn't say. Perhaps he preferred to wait and let you tell me.'

She knew her barb—her charge of hiding behind a woman's skirts—had gone home by the tightening of his lips.

Laura was looking uncomfortable, and David angry, but Deborah felt oddly convinced that his anger was on her mother's behalf rather than his own.

His attitude towards Laura was considerate, protective, and there was a warmth and affection between them that made Deborah feel as though she was on the outside looking in.

But during the last three years he had obviously been here, with her family, on the spot when they needed him, whilst she had stayed away.

Though why should *she* feel guilty? It was *his* fault that she had distanced herself as she had.

To break the awkward silence, Laura hurried into speech. 'But to get back to what I started to tell you—this is one of the suites to accommodate family members who want to stay with a patient in special care. There's a nicely stocked kitchen, and an *en suite* bedroom with twin beds. David has organised a cot, and Kathy and I plan to take it in turns to look after the babe and be with Paul. As soon as the nurse has done I'm going to sit with him until Kathy's finished feeding and changing young Michael.'

'I don't see how the pair of you can cope alone,' Deborah said worriedly. 'Neither of you are properly fit. Kathy can't be back to herself yet, and you're still using a walking frame.'

'Kathy says she's fine, and I'm only using the frame because I promised Alan I would. I can manage quite well without it. But you know how men fuss.'

'Suppose the pair of you need help? I could be here to—'

'No, I won't hear of it,' Laura broke in firmly. 'You go and get a good night's sleep, my love. You look as if you need it.'

'I don't know yet where I'm staying. I just haven't thought about it.'

'You're staying at Thornton Court, of course. Where else would you stay? Benjie is expecting you...'

Thornton had been the family home, and Mrs Benjamin their faithful housekeeper when Richard Hartley had been alive. Both Paul and Deborah had been born and raised there.

After their father's death, and their mother's subsequent remarriage, Paul had taken over the house in Lowry Square, saying he had a fondness for the place and that it was convenient for the office.

'It'll be nice for her to have someone to talk to,' Laura went on. 'I imagine she's been lonely these past few days.' Then, getting back to the nitty-gritty, 'Now, don't you worry. Kathy and I will manage very well between us. And if any problems do crop up there's plenty of help at hand.'

She turned to the door, then hesitated, looking a bit apprehensive—as if the wait had undermined her confidence, made her scared of what she might find.

'I'll come through with you for just a minute,' David said quickly.

Giving him a swift, grateful glance, Laura turned to her

daughter and suggested, 'While David lends me a bit of moral support, why don't you say hello to Kathy and your new nephew?'

As the other two disappeared, Deborah tapped at the bedroom door and called, a shade hesitantly, 'Kathy? It's me...'

'Come on in.'

Deborah obeyed, and found her sister-in-law sitting in a chair feeding the baby.

Kathy was pretty and petite, with dark curly hair and hazel eyes. Frank and good-natured, without a nasty bone in her body, she was everyone's favourite.

Considering all she'd been through in the past few days, she looked remarkably well, Deborah thought, and saluted the spirit that had kept her going.

All she could see of her nephew was a fluff of soft fair hair and a tiny, pink starfish hand spread possessively on his mother's breast.

She felt a strange tug at her heartstrings.

'Hi! Thanks for coming,' Kathy said as Deborah took a seat opposite. 'When Laura and I got to the hospital they told us that since you've been with Paul his condition has started to improve.'

'Yes, thank God. I'm only sorry I—'

'Before you start apologising,' Kathy went on in her forthright way, 'I know the score. And believe me, I don't blame you in the slightest.'

'All the same, these last few days must have been terrible for you.'

'When the accident first happened I was distraught, but David's been an absolute tower of strength. As well as giving us every support he's taken over the running of the company.'

'Yes, Mum said.'

Apparently picking up Deborah's lack of enthusiasm,

Kathy added, 'I'm only too glad he'd do it. It could prove to be a very tricky time.'

'I know Paul mentioned the possibility of a hostile take-over. But surely as things are they wouldn't—?'

'Don't kid yourself,' Kathy said darkly. 'There's no sentiment in business. Crofts will use any dirty trick in the book to get their hands on Hartleys.'

'But Paul seemed to think he had plenty of financial backing.'

'Well, of course he has—thanks to David. But it's much more complicated than that,' Kathy revealed.

'In what way?' Deborah queried.

'If Paul had kept at least fifty-one per cent of shares in the family Hartleys would be safe. But in the early days, before David stepped in, he was forced to sell a large block, and that's left the company dangerously vulnerable. As soon as news of the accident got around share prices began to fall. Which means that some of the shareholders might get worried and begin to offload. But it's not all bad news,' she added with an attempt at cheerfulness. 'We've a big foreign deal in the offing, and if David can manage to pull it off it will restore confidence.'

'What if he can't?' asked Deborah worriedly.

'Share prices are bound to tumble even further, and panic selling could mean big trouble. As far as Crofts are concerned it would be a heaven-sent opportunity for a coup. That is if they didn't have David to deal with. He'll be more than a match for them.' Kathy's faith in her brother was unshakable.

Sitting the baby up, she rubbed his back briefly. 'Now, as I can't wait to see Paul, I'm going to hand your nephew over to you to wind and change.'

Suiting the action to the words, she added, 'As you're getting married, it'll be good practice. Everything you'll need is in the bag over there. When you've finished, put him down in the cot for a sleep. Luckily he's a good little soul, and I dare say Laura will be back soon to keep an eye on him. Now, be sure to get a good night's sleep. You look tired out…'

Touched that Kathy was concerned about *her* at a time like this, Deborah asked, 'Are you certain you and Mum can manage?'

'Quite certain. Will you be coming in tomorrow?'

'Yes, of course.'

'Then use my car. You'll find a spare house key and the car keys in the top drawer of the bureau. That way it'll leave David free to go into the office.'

With a sigh of relief, Deborah said, 'In that case I'll be with you straight after breakfast.'

Giving her sister-in-law a grateful smile, Kathy said, 'Thanks,' and went through to see her husband.

As she supported her nephew with one hand and rubbed his back with the other, while he got his wind up, Deborah studied the tiny scrap.

He was beautiful, with dark blue eyes, perfect little features, and a peachlike down on his flawless skin.

Soon, his head lolling, ridiculously long lashes lying on his plump cheeks, he was more than half asleep. Warm and contented, he smelt of primrose soap and powder, of mother's milk and baby oil.

Again came that tug at her heartstrings, and she thought of the time when she would sit and nurse her own child.

If only Gerald would agree to have a family.

When she had first mentioned having children, looking taken aback, he had said, 'You're a career woman through and through. I can't see children fitting into our kind of lifestyle.'

Just at that moment neither could she, but, unwilling to rule out the possibility, she had persisted, 'I wouldn't like to get married without the hope of having a family one day.'

'If life stays as exciting as it is now, you may change your mind.'

'What if I don't?'

Sighing, he'd said, 'Oh, well, if the worst comes to the worst we can always hire a nanny and soundproof the nursery,' then smiled as though he was joking.

But maybe, knowing she wouldn't accept an outright refusal, he'd only said that to put her off?

When Paul was out of danger and she'd had time to think, and if she decided to forgive and forget and go ahead with the wedding, perhaps she should pin Gerald down? Get a definite promise?

Surely when the time came, he would enjoy being a father? Having someone new and special in his life?

Or would he?

Whether it was just his nature, or because, as an only child, he'd had no one to share things with, Gerald tended to be very self-centred.

It was a fault she knew and accepted. After all, who didn't have faults?

Sighing a little, Deborah addressed her nephew. 'Come on then, young man. Let's have you changed.'

Made awkward by lack of experience, and the fear of dropping him, it took her a moment or two to unfold the changing mat and lay him on it.

As she put him down he woke up and began to kick his little legs and squirm vigorously.

She had disposed of his damp nappy and was down on her knees struggling to fit a clean one when David appeared in the doorway.

Her cheeks flushed, some tendrils of silky hair escaping and a liberal amount of baby powder on her dress, she glanced up at him.

'How very sweet and domesticated you look,' he observed sardonically.

His mockery stung, but, determined not to rise to the bait, Deborah gritted her teeth and returned to her task. But, apparently deciding he'd had enough of being messed about, the baby began to squirm even more and then to cry loudly.

She wondered how something that small could produce so much noise.

Afraid of doing up the nappy too tightly, and made nervous by the rising crescendo of screams—and the knowledge that David was watching her with cynical amusement—she fastened it too loosely, so that when she picked the baby up it dropped round his ankles.

David laughed.

Losing her temper, she challenged, 'If you're so clever, you do it!'

Without hesitation he knelt, and to her great chagrin did it perfectly the first time.

Then, picking the baby up, he put him on his shoulder and patted his back. As if by magic the crying stopped, and a moment later the tiny bundle was being safely tucked up in his cot.

Surprised by the gentle yet confident way David handled the child, she was watching silently when, with a glinting look, he asked, 'Impressed?'

'It would be hard not to be,' she admitted, as she wiped the changing mat and put it back in the bag.

'All anyone needs is a little experience,' he said, as they went through to the bathroom to wash their hands. 'Emily has three-month-old twins.'

Of course. Paul had mentioned that Kathy and her elder sister had both been pregnant at the same time, and, hearing of the birth, Deborah had sent a card congratulating the proud parents.

She brushed the powder from her dress, and was tucking in the stray tendrils of hair when, his tone derisive, David added, 'Kathy said you were getting your hand in, but I can't imagine that you and Delcy have any room for babies in your career-orientated designer lives.'

His words cut like knife slashes.

Before she could tell him he was wrong, at least in her case, Laura appeared in the doorway.

'I'm back. Everything all right?'

'Fine,' David assured her.

'What did Paul's latest check show?' Deborah asked.

'It's good news...' Laura's voice shook a little. 'The improvement is being maintained.'

The two women hugged each other thankfully. Both had tears in their eyes.

Turning to David, Laura said, 'We're so pleased and relieved to be able to stay with him. I don't know how to thank you.'

'There's no need for thanks,' he told her, adding, 'You'll find your charge is fast asleep, so we'll get off and you can put your feet up for a while.'

Deborah kissed her mother, and, trying to hide her weariness, said, 'Promise that if you need me you'll let me know?'

'I promise. Though I'm quite sure that Kathy and I will manage fine.'

'If there's any change...' Deborah said.

'We'll ring you at once.'

'Take care not to overdo things,' David said, 'and we'll see you tomorrow.'

'Kathy's offered to loan Deborah her car, so if you want to go straight into the office...?'

'If everything's all right, I may do that.'

Outside, it was no longer damp and overcast. A front had moved through, bringing cooler weather and a brisk north-easterly wind.

Shivering a little, Deborah accompanied David back to the car and, recalling his kindness to her mother, made an effort to be pleasant. 'I hope dropping me off at Lowry Square won't take you too far out of your way?'

'No, not at all,' he answered coolly.

When she had first met him he had had a flat in Mayfair, but now she had no idea where he lived or who he lived with—whether he was in a steady relationship or even married.

But a man who attracted women like buddleia attracted butterflies would hardly be living alone.

When they got back to the car he helped her in. Then sliding in beside her, reached across to fasten her seatbelt.

Every nerve in her body clamouring, she froze, paralysed by his close proximity and the uncomfortable knowledge that, in spite of everything, the old sexual attraction was still there.

It would be a great relief when he had dropped her off and she could get away from his disturbing presence and be alone with her thoughts.

'Comfortable?' he asked smoothly.

'Yes, thank you,' she mumbled.

So much had happened in such a short time that she felt physically and emotionally drained. Unwilling to talk, she leaned back and closed her eyes.

Within seconds she was fast asleep.

She slept soundly until they reached the charming cul-de-sac where Kathy and Paul lived, then, apparently wakened by some sixth sense, opened her eyes to the familiar scene.

Lowry Square had an oblong iron-railing-enclosed area in the centre, with gravel paths, a few shady trees, a dolphin fountain, and a scattering of slatted benches. Now it was full of spring flowers.

It was bordered by short terraces of townhouses and Thornton Court itself, which stood alone on the far side of the quiet square, its walled garden backing on to the leafy greenness of Lowry Park.

To the right of the wrought-iron gates stood a coach-house that had been turned into garages, and to the left, between the main gates and the tradesmen's entrance, a small lodge where the housekeeper lived.

The gates had been left open, and David drove in and up the short drive to the paved apron in front of the house.

It was a square Georgian building, with uniform windows and variegated ivy growing up its redbrick walls. A short flight of steps guarded by wrought-iron rails led up to an oak door over which a large lantern hung, casting a pool of yellow light in the gathering blue dusk.

A noisy flock of birds appeared, and were blown about like pieces of black litter in the windy sky before coming to roost in the tall trees.

Getting out of the car, Deborah gave an involuntary sigh. Though she hadn't seen her old family home for over three years, nothing had changed. It still gave the impression of being in some pleasant country town rather than in the heart of London.

David was lifting her case from the boot when the grey-haired, neatly dressed housekeeper opened the door. 'So you're here at last! How nice to see you, Miss Deborah.'

'It's nice to see you, Benjie. How are you?'

'Mustn't grumble. Though I've missed Oscar since he died a couple of months ago.'

Remembering how fond Mrs Benjamin had been of the old black Labrador, Deborah suggested, 'Why don't you get another dog?'

'Mr Paul suggested that. But I couldn't start again with a puppy at my age.' Turning, she led the way into the spacious hall.

Carrying her suitcase, David followed them in and closed the door.

Beaming at Deborah, Mrs Benjamin went on, 'Though you live so far away I knew you'd come! Didn't I tell Mrs

Hartley so when she was worrying herself sick? Now, your old room's waiting, and dinner will be ready in about fifteen minutes.'

Though more tired than hungry, Deborah smiled at the thin, garrulous woman and said, 'Thanks, Benjie, that sounds great.'

'How was Mr Paul when you left him?'

'His condition seems to have improved somewhat.'

'Heaven be praised,' the housekeeper cried. 'It's a terrible thing to have happened at a time like this. But he'll be all right. Never you fear. He's not a man to give in.'

Then, with no apparent pause for breath, 'How does Mrs Hartley seem?'

'Better than I'd expected.'

'And the baby?'

'He's absolutely beautiful,' Deborah answered. Adding drily, 'And with plenty of lung power.'

Mrs Benjamin laughed. 'So had his father, if I remember rightly. Though you were always a quiet little thing... To think of you living in New York! What's it like there? I hear it's a fascinating place—'

'Is that our dinner I smell burning?' David's voice, quiet but decisive, cut neatly through the flow of words.

'Lordy me, so it is.' Without more ado, she hurried back to the kitchen.

Bristling at the way he'd dismissed the housekeeper, Deborah said sharply, 'Benjie's been here for over thirty years. You've no right to speak to her like that.'

Unruffled, he stared back at her. 'If you want to talk about New York that's fine by me. But standing in the hall while our meal is getting overcooked hardly seems to be the appropriate time or place.'

Our meal...

'So you're intending to eat here?'

'Yes.'

Seeing the gleam of ironic amusement in his blue eyes, she caught her breath. Surely he wasn't…?

But even as she tried to dismiss the possibility she knew she'd guessed right.

Swallowing, she said almost accusingly, 'You're *staying* here?'

'That's right…'

Why on earth was he staying here? she wondered vexedly. Why not at his own flat?

'I take it you have no objections?'

'As it's Kathy and Paul's house now it's really nothing to do with me,' she informed him stiffly, and she turned and stalked up the stairs.

He followed her and, straight-faced, set her case down just inside her bedroom door.

'Thank you,' she said with frigid politeness.

'About fifteen minutes—OK?'

'I'm not really hungry, and I—'

'If you're not down I'll be up to fetch you,' he stated simply.

Deborah took a sharp breath.

'Of all the domineering, arrogant—'

'You should keep your strength up just in case Kathy and your mother do need you.'

Seeing the sense in that, and knowing he was quite capable of carrying out his threat, she said grudgingly, 'Very well. I'll be down.'

When David had disappeared along the corridor she lifted her case onto the blanket chest and looked around the familiar room, with its happy memories of her childhood and teenage years.

Painted peach, white and apple-green—a simple but charming combination of cool fresh colours—and furnished with the minimum of light modern furniture, it hadn't altered since she'd left it at eighteen to go to college.

But *she* had.

Then, though quiet by nature, she had been sunny and light-hearted. Life had been good to her, and with the blind optimism of youth she had never imagined it being any different.

Her college years had been very happy ones, marred only by the death of her father, who had died from a heart attack at the age of forty-eight.

Then she had met David.

She had been wearing a modest, Maid Marian-style dress she had designed herself at the party, with her long hair plaited into a single thick braid.

At five foot seven, taller than most of her friends, she had always thought of herself as too tall and gawky. But then, finding that David, who easily topped six foot, preferred tall women, she had been glad of her near model-girl height.

He had taken her home after the party, and she had seen him every evening from then on.

She had wanted to be with him all the time. Head over heels in love, she had pinched herself a lot, and smiled when nobody was there.

No one had ever made her feel that way before.

She had been notorious amongst her college friends for *not* sleeping around; ridiculed for being far too romantic; teased for being old-fashioned about sex.

But she had never understood one-night stands or drifting from one bed to another. She thought it relegated the feeling between two people to meaningless lust.

To her, making love was much more than a pleasurable coming together. It was trust and commitment, hopes and dreams and love, as well as shared joy and delight.

Some two months later, on a wet night in September, David had taken her to The Spinning Wheel, and they'd spent a lovely romantic evening dining and dancing by candlelight.

For weeks it had been plain that, though he wanted her, he was holding back, leaving her to make the first move.

But, though she'd wanted him, the knowledge of her own inexperience and the thought that she might disappoint him had been enough to prevent her.

Until that night.

Then, during the smoochy numbers, when he had held her close, she had let her fingers stray to the nape of his neck and into his hair.

Afterwards he had taken her back to his flat for the first time, and she had gone to bed with him without a qualm. He hadn't pushed or pressured her into it; it had simply been where she wanted to be.

'You're absolutely breathtaking,' he had whispered while he slowly undressed her, kissing and tasting each newly uncovered inch of flesh. 'And you just don't know it. You have the loveliest face and body, and not a hint of vanity…'

She had been vaguely aware of the rain beating against the windows, but then she had forgotten that and everything else, except for the touch of his hands and his mouth.

When her last garment had been removed, and she had trembled like a leaf, he had lifted her gently onto the bed and begun to strip off his own clothes. She had watched the light from the standard lamp gilding his body and found him beautiful.

Naked, he had stretched out beside her, then his strong arms had gathered her close and her long legs had wound around his.

CHAPTER FOUR

DISCOVERING that she was totally inexperienced, David had been so gentle, so patient, such a skilful and considerate lover. He'd made it easy for her.

He had seemed to know instinctively what she needed—how to hold her, where to touch her to give her the utmost delight.

Men were selfish, her college friends had told her, all they thought about was their own pleasure. But he had been willing to wait, to hold back, until she was right there with him. And when she had been certain there could be no greater rapture than she had just experienced he had proved her wrong.

Brushing the strands of damp hair away from her cheeks, he had kissed her tenderly. And then, turning her onto her face and cupping her breasts so he could tease the nipples, had gone on to give her such delight she had thought she might die…

Shuddering at the erotic memory, she dragged herself back to the present and, having found a change of clothing, hurried into the bathroom. Already five minutes had elapsed, and she didn't want David to have to come looking for her.

A hot shower dispelled some of her weariness, and physically she began to feel a little better. Mentally, however, she was in a state of turmoil as she towelled herself, dried her hair, and put on fresh undies.

The last thing she wanted was to be in such close contact with David—to be sleeping under the same roof, to have to eat her meals with him, to be forced to toe his line.

To remember how it had once been.

Well, she needn't. If he intended to stay on here, tomorrow she could—and would—move out.

She finished dressing quickly, and, after plaiting her thick silky hair into a loose braid—something she hadn't done for a long time—hurried downstairs.

In spite of her haste, David was already in the dining room, standing by the window looking out into the dusky garden.

Though her feet were silent on the thick carpet, he turned at her approach. He had changed into well-cut trousers and an olive-green shirt, open at the neck. His crisp dark hair, still damp, was trying to curl.

Remembering how it always had after they'd showered together made her throat go dry, and she was forced to swallow hard.

The cool blue eyes studied her, taking in her cream designer jeans and boat-necked top, before lifting leisurely to her clear-skinned face, free of make-up, and the thick rope of ash-blonde hair.

'You look about sixteen,' he commented, 'and as beautiful as ever.'

'I'm so *glad* you approve of how I look,' she told him, with saccharine sweetness.

His eyes glinted. 'Oh, I don't approve. For one thing, you're much too thin.'

'It's fashionable.' She used Gerald's words.

'It may be fashionable, but it doesn't suit you. You're thin to the point of gauntness, and one of the most enticing things about you was your nicely rounded curves. I remember how I could just cup one of your breasts in my palm and—'

Turning on him furiously, she hissed, 'Stop it! Or I'll walk out of here this minute.'

'Dear me,' he murmured mildly. 'You're very touchy these days.'

'And you're—'

At that instant the door opened and Mrs Benjamin wheeled in the dinner trolley. As she began to transfer various dishes to the table she glanced from one to the other, as if picking up the tension.

'There, now. It's a simple enough meal. Just a chicken casserole with some good fresh vegetables, followed by cheese and fruit... I expect you get a lot of fancy food in New York.'

Deborah managed a smile and said, 'We don't get anything better than your casseroles. I remember they were always delicious.'

Gratified, Mrs Benjamin smiled before adding, 'And there's a bottle of chilled white wine, as well as a nice drop of port to go with the cheese. I've often wondered, do they eat much cheese in the States? It seems to me—'

Pulling out a chair for Deborah, David said, 'Thank you, Mrs Benjamin. There's no need to stay. We'll serve ourselves.'

Where did he get his nerve from? Deborah wondered resentfully. Giving orders as if he owned the place...

But the housekeeper nodded calmly. 'Right you are. Just ring when you're ready for coffee.'

When she had gone, David opened and poured the wine, then served Deborah with a generous helping of chicken and vegetables before taking some himself.

Several times he essayed a light remark, but, still ruffled, Deborah answered in monosyllables.

Finally, he asked with a sigh, 'Did you really want to converse with the housekeeper while we ate?'

'I would have liked a choice in the matter.'

'In that case, I'm sorry.'

She gave him a stony look.

'I gather Mrs Benjamin, while a very worthy woman, has always been in the habit of chatting.'

'What if she has? It still doesn't excuse you being so abominably rude to her.'

'If I came over as rude, I'm sorry. It wasn't intentional. However, it doesn't alter the fact that if nothing's done to curb that habit it could get worse as she gets older. She could start making a complete nuisance of herself.'

'Isn't that a bit over-dramatic? After all, she isn't some kind of monster. I expect she's just lonely since her old dog died.'

'I hadn't appreciated—'

'I'm sure you hadn't. You have to be human to appreciate that people can be lonely and in need of some company.'

She saw his jaw tighten, but he said nothing, and, returning her attention to her plate, she ate in frosty silence.

Uptight, she couldn't wait for the uncomfortable meal to be over. But a surreptitious glance at her companion's face suggested he had regained his composure and was perfectly at ease again.

Advantage to him, she thought sourly.

But this would be the last time.

'Cheese?' he enquired pleasantly, when their plates were empty.

'No, thank you.' She was forced to stifle a yawn.

'You look ready for bed,' he commented.

'I'm more than ready.'

'Then I'll ring the bell for coffee.'

Remembering all he'd done, and striving to be fair, she remarked, 'You must be tired too?'

He surprised her by admitting simply, 'I am.'

Mrs Benjamin arrived promptly. 'Here we are. Nice and fresh and hot.' Setting the tray down, she hastened away without another word.

'There—you see,' Deborah said accusingly. 'You've obviously hurt her feelings.'

'I doubt it. She's probably hurrying back to look at some soap or other on television.'

Annoyed afresh by his callous indifference, she asked abruptly, 'How long will you be staying here?'

'I'm not sure,' he answered casually. 'Does it make any difference?'

'It does to me.'

A gleam in his eye, he assured her, 'Well, if you want me to, I'll certainly stay.'

'I *don't* want you to. In fact if you're intending to stay I shall move out.'

'I think not.'

'What do you mean?'

'I mean you *won't* be moving out.'

Losing her temper, she cried, 'Who the devil do you think you are, giving me orders? Let me tell you I don't take orders from anyone—least of all you! I shall move into a hotel tomorrow.'

Jumping to her feet, she stormed out of the room and up the stairs.

As she reached her bedroom door, quick, light footsteps sounded behind her, and steely fingers closed about her wrist, jerking her round.

'You'll do no such thing. I won't have Kathy and your mother harassed any more.'

'I don't know what you mean.'

His blue eyes blazed. 'You know perfectly well what I mean. If you insist on moving into a hotel it will only upset them both.'

'I'm sorry, but—'

'And if you hurt either Laura's or Kathy's feelings you'll have me to answer to.'

'How very noble and gallant you are,' she taunted, and turned away.

She was swung back and pinned none too gently against

the heavy oak door. Then, his thumb and fingers holding either side of her face, he forced her head up.

'Not to all women,' he told her silkily. 'Not to women like you, for example.'

Her green eyes widened with shock.

'Kathy and your mother have got quite enough on their plates without a selfish little brat like you worrying them.'

His strong fingers slipped first to the warm vulnerability of her throat and then slid down under the neckline of her top, to very lightly brush the upper swells of her breasts with just his sensitive fingertips. 'Now, I suggest you forget about moving out, or I might be tempted to show you just how *ungallant* I can be.'

She swallowed convulsively, unable to suppress a shiver of pleasure at his touch, and he smiled a little, as if satisfied. The next moment she was free, and he was disappearing back down the corridor, lithe and graceful for so big a man.

Shaken, Deborah stood for some seconds without moving. Then, rage bringing a flush to her cheeks, she told herself furiously that she hated him. That as soon as Paul was out of danger she'd go back to the States and never come within a mile of David again.

Once in her room, having found her nightdress and sponge bag, she showered, brushed her hair and cleaned her teeth before climbing into bed.

Despite her weariness, however, she was unable to settle, the rush of adrenaline and the turmoil of her thoughts keeping her wide awake and restless.

Next morning, after a virtually sleepless night, she stayed in her room until she was sure David had gone, then ventured downstairs.

Mrs Benjamin made her fresh toast and coffee and fussed over her, saying how tired and wan she looked, putting her lack of sleep down to worrying about her brother.

'But there's no need to fret,' that good lady went on placidly. 'Before Mr David left for the office he phoned the hospital, and Mr Paul's doing fine.'

Surprised to hear David referred to in the same manner as Paul, Deborah asked, 'How do you get on with…David?'

'Very well,' Mrs Benjamin answered cheerfully.

'You don't resent him giving you orders?'

'Why, bless your heart, no. I've known Mr David a long time. He's a nice young man—always fair, a good friend to Mr Paul, and devoted to his sister. And one time when I needed some help he…'

Having started the ball rolling, Deborah was forced to listen to a eulogy on how kind David was before she could escape.

When she reached the hospital, the good news was confirmed. Paul had regained consciousness and was sleeping naturally.

'He's young and resilient,' Dr Hezelden told them. 'And now he's got this far he should be off the critical list in a day or so.'

All three women were elated.

Deborah sat with him throughout the morning while Kathy and her mother had a break. Though Paul slept most of the time, on a couple of occasions he opened his eyes and looked at her before drifting off again.

At twelve o'clock Kathy took over, while the baby slept soundly in his cot and Deborah and her mother ate lunch.

Over a simple meal of honey-roast ham and salad, Laura asked cautiously, 'How are things going? With David, I mean?'

Unwilling to worry her mother, Deborah answered mendaciously, 'Everything's fine.'

'I see.' Laura sighed.

'All right, so it's not.' Deborah remembered his behaviour

of the previous night and her voice shook a little. 'He's impossible! He's cold and hard and arrogant…'

'If at times he seems cold and hard and arrogant…well, you must know he isn't really like that. He's warm and sensitive, and more considerate than almost any man I've ever known,' Laura defended.

'He might be considerate to you and Kathy, but he certainly isn't to me.'

'Well, my love, your rejection did hurt him very much. When you broke the engagement he was quite devastated. It took him a long time to get over it.'

Deborah bit back a bitter denouncement. Even after more than three years she couldn't bring herself to tell her mother the sorry truth.

'By the way…' Laura sounded almost apologetic. 'When he popped in again last night to make sure we were coping—'

'He came in again last night?'

'Yes, it was quite late… He said he'd call in at lunchtime today.'

Jumping to her feet, Deborah said quickly, 'Well, if it's all the same to you, I'll get off.'

'Look, love, you don't have to go just because—'

'I've some phone calls to make, and this is a good time to do it. I'll be able to catch Gerald and Fran before they leave for work. See you this afternoon.'

She dropped a quick kiss on her mother's cheek and hurried away, breathing a sigh of relief when she left the hospital grounds without running into David.

Back at Thornton Court, she rang her flatmate and gave her a brief update. 'Though Paul's not out of danger yet, he's regained consciousness…'

'That's great news!' Fran exclaimed. 'I bet you're all so relieved… Have you spoken to Gerald yet?'

'No.' Though she knew she must, not quite knowing what to say, she had put it off until last.

'Well, be prepared. He doesn't feel any shame for not telling you about your brother, and he's hopping mad that you left without a word.'

'Thanks for the warning.'

'Is the wedding still on?'

'I'm not sure,' Deborah said slowly. 'I haven't really had a chance to think things over yet.'

'Well, I know one thing,' Fran said stoutly. 'Even if I loved him, I wouldn't marry anyone who could be so unfeeling.' Then, quickly, 'Sorry—I shouldn't have said that. Of course you must make up your own mind.'

'When I do, I'll let you know. Take care, now.'

'And you. I hope everything goes well for your brother. I'll keep saying my prayers.'

Thinking what a good friend Fran was, Deborah braced herself and rang Gerald's apartment.

Plainly in a bad mood, he answered curtly, 'Delcy.'

'It's me.'

'Where the devil are you?'

'I'm in London. Surely Fran told you?'

'She told me you'd gone off half-cocked with some man or other.' Sounding aggrieved, he went on, 'How *could* you go rushing off without a word when we're due to be married on Saturday?'

'How could *you* let me go through a whole weekend without telling me that Paul was critically ill?' Deborah came back angrily.

'I didn't see any point in ruining all our plans. And what difference would it have made whether you were there or not?'

'My being here would have made a great deal of difference—especially to Mum and Kathy. Even if it hadn't,

Paul's my brother, and I *wanted* to be here. You had no right to keep it from me,' Deborah snapped.

His voice sulky now, Gerald said, 'I only did it for the best. There's no need to sound as if I committed some heinous crime. After all, you're not *that* close to your family.'

'We've always been extremely close,' she insisted, with spirit.

'You told me yourself that you'd seen hardly anything of them in the past three years. And when we visited it was obvious you no longer had anything in common. You were relieved to get back to New York.'

She was forced to admit that most of what he said was true. In all fairness it might well have been her own attitude that had made him think she didn't care.

'So I absolutely refuse to be blamed,' he was going on petulantly. 'In fact I believe *I'm* the injured party. I felt a perfect fool when that supercilious flatmate of yours rang me…'

'I'm sorry.'

Her apology failed to stop the flow. 'I'm not used to being treated as if I'm of no account. You went off without so much as a word, with no indication of when you were coming back—'

Gritting her teeth, she broke in, 'If all's well, I'm hoping to be back by Friday at the latest.'

'Damn it, Deborah, it's just not good enough. I want you to come home *today*.'

'I'm afraid I can't do that.'

'I *insist* that you return home immediately. If you want this wedding to go ahead as planned you'd better listen to what—'

Angry because he hadn't even asked how Paul was, she cut the threat off short. 'I'm no longer sure if I want to marry you.'

For a second or two there was complete silence, then he

rushed into panicky speech. 'But all the arrangements are made. It's far too late to change your mind now. What will all my…our friends say?'

He'd been right the first time, she found herself thinking. Nearly all 'their' friends were *his* friends. The only person she could really count as a friend was Fran.

'I would be sorry to hurt your family, but apart from that I don't much care what anyone says,' she informed him flatly.

'Look, darling…' his tone was placatory now '…I know you must be stressed at the moment, and I don't want to quarrel—'

'Neither do I,' she said quickly. 'But I have no intention of coming back until Paul's out of danger.'

'How are things going?' Gerald asked grudgingly.

'He's regained consciousness and seems to be making good progress. Even so, it'll be a day or two before he's off the critical list.'

'But you will be back Friday?' Gerald pressed.

'I hope to be.' She refused to commit herself.

'You didn't mean what you said about not wanting to marry me?'

'I said I wasn't sure, and I'm not. The whole thing may be a big mistake. I need time to think about it.'

He cleared his throat, and, fearing more pressure, she told him quickly, 'I must get back to the hospital now. I'll ring you as soon as I've any positive news.'

'I hope everything goes well.' He sounded almost humble. 'Take care of yourself, darling.'

'And you.'

She was about to replace the receiver when suddenly, fiercely, he said, 'I miss you. Please come home soon.'

Thinking of David's harshness, she admitted, 'I can't wait to be home.'

* * *

During the next couple of days, Deborah contrived to avoid her *bête noire* completely. The mornings were no problem. David got up, breakfasted early, and left the house well before eight. Not until he was safely out of the way did she venture downstairs.

She dodged his lunchtime visits to the hospital, ate dinner with Kathy and her mother, and when she got back to Thornton Court slipped in by the side entrance and crept straight up to her room.

Though still sleeping a good deal of the time, in between naps—to everyone's great relief—Paul was wide awake and able to converse for short periods.

On Wednesday morning he'd been able to see his baby son for the first time. It had been an emotional moment. Later that day he'd asked how things were at Hartleys, and been assured that everything was fine.

After dinner on Thursday evening, when both Paul and the baby were asleep and Deborah was about to leave for home, came the news they had all been hoping and praying for.

Beaming at the three women, Dr Hezelden confirmed that Paul had been taken off the critical list. 'From now on it's just a matter of careful nursing...'

Tears of relief in their eyes, Kathy, Laura and Deborah hugged each other.

Sniffing a little, Kathy queried, 'Does that mean we should vacate the apartment?'

'No, not at all. It's yours for as long as you want to stay.'

When the doctor had gone, Kathy turned to her sister-in-law and said, 'You've been an absolute brick. I can't thank you enough for all your help and support. I realise just how much it must have cost you, so now Paul's out of danger please feel free to go back to the States as soon as you like.'

She glanced at her mother-in-law, as though hoping for some backing. Getting no response, she went on seriously,

'I don't want you to have to postpone your wedding. If you went back tomorrow, even though it will be a terrible rush for you, everything could go ahead as planned, couldn't it?'

'Will it be possible to get a flight at such short notice?' Laura asked.

Deborah was about to say that finding a single seat shouldn't be a problem when Kathy said, 'Don't be silly, Mum. David will take care of everything. I'll mention it to him when he—'

'No, don't,' Deborah broke in quickly. 'I haven't decided yet exactly what I'm doing. I need some time to think.'

Neither of the other women said anything, but Deborah noticed that her mother looked relieved.

'Well, I'd better get off home now. If I *do* decide to go tomorrow, and I haven't time to come in again, take care of yourselves. Give Paul my love, and the babe a kiss.'

On the way back to Thornton Court, Deborah made an effort to get her thoughts into some kind of order. For the past two or three days, unable to think or plan ahead, she'd been living in a kind of vacuum, just waiting. But now Paul was out of danger she had some serious decisions to make.

She wanted to get back to New York and away from David as soon as possible, but she was still in two minds about the wedding.

If it hadn't been for Paul's accident—and it was nothing to do with meeting David again, she told herself firmly—she would have got married without any hesitation.

But seeing Gerald in a new and not so pleasant light had unsettled her, shaken her faith in their future together and made her have second thoughts.

Though now Paul was going to be fine surely she could let bygones be bygones and go ahead with the wedding as planned?

Apart from David, Gerald was the only man who had ever

seriously attracted her—the only man she had ever loved and wanted to marry.

But did she still love him?

She was no longer certain.

A fresh thought shook her. Had she really loved him in the first place? Or had she merely been dazzled by his good looks and sophisticated charm?

No, surely she must have loved him. She had always believed that love and marriage went hand in hand; if she hadn't loved him she would never have agreed to marry him.

So if she had loved him once, she probably still did. Then why was she hesitating? She *would* marry him, and have her glittering future just as she'd visualised it.

Her mind made up, she resolved that as soon as she reached Thornton Court she would ring Gerald and tell him she loved him and would be back home in time for the wedding.

She waited for the feeling of relief that should automatically have followed her decision.

It failed to arrive. Instead she was back to feeling wretchedly uncertain. Would going ahead with the wedding prove to be a terrible mistake?

When she reached Thornton Court she was still on a see-saw of indecision.

As she turned into the tradesmen's entrance she saw Mrs Benjamin, approaching the lodge with a liver-and-white Springer spaniel on a lead.

Stopping the car, Deborah got out to tell her the good news about Paul.

'Heaven be praised!' the housekeeper exclaimed. 'I just knew everything would be all right. Does that mean Mrs Hartley will be coming home?'

'I think she and Mum will be staying at the hospital for

a while longer. But no doubt they'll let you know exactly what their plans are.'

'If you need anything tonight, Miss Deborah, I'll come back to the house...'

'Not a thing, thanks, Benjie.'

'Well, as you've been staying at the hospital to eat, and Mr David's taken to going straight out again after dinner—I expect he needs a break—I thought I might as well take Tammy for a walk in the park.'

Well, everyone was entitled to some social life, Deborah thought, but if she'd known David wasn't home in the evenings she needn't have gone to so much trouble to avoid him.

Stooping to stroke the spaniel, whose tail was going like a metronome, she asked, 'Who does Tammy belong to?'

'She's mine,' Mrs Benjamin said proudly. 'Mr David gave her to me...'

It seemed he could be nice to everyone but her.

'When he suggested getting me another dog, I told him I couldn't cope with training a puppy. So he found me Tammy, who's a year old and already fully trained. Bless her heart, she's so good-natured and clever—and isn't it nice that her tail's not docked? Her previous owner is going to live abroad and can't take her, so she needed a caring home. I only got her this afternoon, but she's settled in already. We're having some milk and arrowroot biscuits when we get in—aren't we, lovey?'

The Springer wagged her tail even harder.

'There—see!' Mrs Benjamin exclaimed triumphantly, 'She understands every word I say. Now, you're quite sure you don't need anything, Miss Deborah?'

'Quite sure, thanks. When I've made some phone calls I intend to go straight to bed. I'm hoping to fly back to the States tomorrow...'

'In time for the wedding? Well, if that's what you want

I hope you'll be very happy. What about breakfast? Will you need—?'

'Don't worry about breakfast. If I can book an early flight, I'll get something at the airport,' Deborah said.

'Well, take care of yourself, Miss Deborah.'

'And you.' Deborah gave the elderly housekeeper an affectionate hug.

Having let herself into the house, she stood, hesitating, then, still with no clear idea of what she was going to say, she picked up the phone and dialled Gerald's number.

It was a relief when, after it had rung for a little while, an answering machine cut in.

Avoiding all mention of the wedding, she kept it short and sweet. 'Gerald, it's Deborah. Paul's off the critical list, thank God, so I'm hoping to be back tomorrow. I'll get in touch in the morning and let you know which flight I'm on. Bye for now.'

Next she rang the airport, and after some slight delay managed to book a seat on a plane which, because of the time difference, would get her into JFK quite early the following day.

That done, she went upstairs and repacked her case. Then, having set the alarm for six o'clock, to make sure she would be away well before David came down, she undressed and showered and climbed wearily into bed.

Perhaps she'd be able to make a final positive decision about the wedding when she'd had a good night's sleep.

But sleep eluded her.

After tossing and turning for several hours, at half past twelve she threw in her hand and, in her thin satin nightdress, her ash-blonde hair tumbling round her shoulders, padded barefoot down the stairs to make herself a hot drink.

Despite all its mod cons, the kitchen was still homely and warm and comfortable—a nice place to be. With its scrubbed-oak table, and a cushioned rocking-chair each side of the Aga, it had changed little since her childhood days.

Pegged rugs still lay on the tiled floor, and the window-seats were still covered in the same floral-patterned material as the curtains.

It was here that, on wet days, she and Paul had played and talked and told each other their secrets. Instead of being scolded or frowned at for getting under Mrs Benjamin's feet, they had been welcomed and fed biscuits and milk and homemade fairy cakes at the old oak table.

Smiling a little at the happy memories, Deborah found a tin of drinking chocolate and a mug. She had just taken a bottle of milk from the fridge and removed the cap when some sixth sense made her glance round.

David stood in the doorway, a navy blue towelling robe belted round his lean waist, his bare feet thrust into mules. The robe was open at the neck, showing the strong column of his throat and an expanse of smooth, muscular chest.

'Not able to sleep?' he asked mildly.

Trying to hide her sudden panic, she said, 'No. I thought I'd make a cup of hot chocolate.'

He closed the door and, crossing the kitchen to stand beside the Aga, ordered laconically, 'Make it two—I've been wanting to talk to you.'

She felt a strong urge to turn and run, but, unwilling to behave like a scared rabbit, made herself stay where she was.

His hair was rumpled and a little damp, as though he'd recently showered, and with his eyes gleaming, and his jaw darkened by a new growth of beard, he looked virile and sexy—almost irresistible…

Realising the treachery of her thoughts, she bit her lip and, needing something to say, asked, 'Can't you sleep either?'

'I've just got in.'

'Been painting the town? Don't worry,' she added sarcastically, reaching for another mug, 'I'm sure both Mum and Kathy will feel you've earned a bit of social life.'

Out of the corner of her eye she saw him move towards her. Suddenly scared, she flinched away, dropping the mug and knocking the milk bottle over.

The mug broke neatly in two, and milk ran over the work surface and dripped onto the floor.

David righted the bottle quickly and, his hand gripping her elbow, steered her to the nearest chair. 'You'd better sit down before you do any more damage. Anyone would think you were nervous of me,' he added, his face sardonic.

Looking anywhere but at him, yet still conscious of his every movement, Deborah gritted her teeth and said nothing.

Deftly and efficiently he disposed of the broken mug, mopped up the mess, heated two mugs of milk and spooned in the chocolate.

All desire for a hot drink had vanished, and, very conscious of her bare legs and the flimsiness of her nightdress, Deborah's only thought was to get it over with as quickly as possible.

CHAPTER FIVE

'I HAVEN'T seen much of you lately,' David remarked. 'I'd begun to think you were avoiding me.'

'I've been fairly late leaving the hospital,' she said with perfect truth. Then, gladly, 'There was some good news to-night...'

'Yes, I know.'

'Did Kathy call you?'

'No.' His chiselled mouth twisted in the semblance of a smile. 'I've taken to popping into the hospital quite late on my way home from Hartleys.'

'You been working every evening?'

'It's been necessary while I've been trying to push that foreign deal through.'

Deborah cringed inwardly, feeling very much in the wrong. She had accused him of painting the town when in fact he'd been working to save her brother's firm.

'I'm sorry,' she began. 'I shouldn't have presumed you were—'

He shook his head. 'It doesn't matter.'

But it did.

'How is the deal going?' she forced herself to ask.

'I've only got to sign the contract.'

'That's great.' She was genuinely pleased—not only for Paul's sake, but that Kathy's touching faith in her brother had been justified.

'Here we are.' Handing her a steaming mug, and taking his own, David sat down in the chair opposite and observed softly, 'Now, isn't this cosy?'

For some reason the apparently innocent remark made every nerve in her body tighten with apprehension.

She drank half her hot chocolate as quickly as possible, then, rising to her feet, put her mug on the table. 'I'll be getting back to bed.'

The next second David's mug was beside her own, and his tall, broad-shouldered figure was barring her way. 'What's the hurry?' he asked lazily.

She was overwhelmingly aware of his aura of vital masculinity. Her heart starting to race, she stepped backwards, making an attempt to go round him.

Lean fingers closed lightly about her wrist, but she guessed that if she made any move to break free his grip would tighten.

Made a prisoner by her own apprehension, she hesitated, head bent, the lamp casting the shadow of her long lashes onto her cheeks.

Just that light touch was having a devastating effect on her, and, her heart thudding so loudly she thought he must hear it, she said, 'I'd like to go.'

Slowly, caressingly, his thumb began to stroke across the inside of her wrist. 'We haven't finished our talk.'

'I don't think there's anything to talk about,' she informed him stiffly. 'Unless you're waiting for me to thank you for getting Benjie a dog.'

'I wasn't. But if you're determined to thank me, a kiss will do nicely.'

'Please, David…'

She was very conscious of his nearness, of his imposing height and the breadth of his shoulders, of the small, seductive movements his thumb was continuing to make.

In a sudden panic, she tried to break free.

As she had suspected, he refused to allow it. Her heart gave a lurch, then began to beat again at an even more frantic rate.

He raised her hand and brushed his lips over the warm silky skin of her inner wrist.

Shivering, she begged, 'Don't do that,' and, snatching her hand free, she put it flat-palmed against his chest, as if to hold him away.

He placed his own well-shaped hand over hers, pinning it to his heart.

After a moment he remarked softly, 'You're trembling. Anyone would think you were scared of me.'

'Then anyone would be wrong,' she retorted, with a fine show of spirit.

'In that case why don't you sit down again and finish your hot chocolate?'

Seeing he wasn't going to let her go until he was good and ready, she reluctantly obeyed.

When she remained stubbornly silent, he asked conversationally, 'Now Paul's out of danger, are you thinking of returning to the States?'

'Of course.'

'How soon were you hoping to leave?'

'Tomorrow.'

'Then I'll let Luther Johnson, my pilot, know.'

'Thank you, but there's no need,' she broke in quickly. 'I'm already booked on a flight.'

'I see. What time does it leave?'

Reluctantly, she told him.

'So the wedding's still on?'

She hesitated, then said hardily, 'Of course it is. Why shouldn't it be?'

'Well, if you *want* to marry a man like Delcy…' His voice was caustic. 'Or is it simply to consolidate your career?'

'No, it isn't. I happen to love Gerald.'

'In spite of his faults?'

'No one's perfect.'

'True. But some faults are much easier to live with than others,' he said.

'I'm sure you're right. Gerald may be blinkered and self-centred, but he isn't callous or unfaithful,' Deborah said pointedly.

'Do you really believe that?'

'Yes, I do,' she retorted shortly.

'Don't you consider it callous of him not to tell you about Paul?' he queried, almost idly.

'He presumed we were no longer close.'

'Quite a presumption to make,' David said silkily.

'In a way it was justified.'

'How do you make that out?'

'He knew I hadn't been home for three years, and he drew his own conclusions. Now, if you don't mind, I'm going to bed,' Deborah stated, wanting to escape from the interrogation.

David rose, and, collecting the empty mugs, said a shade mockingly, 'When I've dealt with these I'll see you upstairs.'

Though she was desperate to get away, she felt oddly certain that he would prevent any move to leave without him.

In spite of all her efforts she found herself peeping at him surreptitiously, watching the way he washed and dried the mugs.

She had always been fascinated by the movements of his hands. The way he tied his shoelaces, combed his hair, shaved. So masculine, yet so deft and elegant.

From the start she had wanted to experience all those hands could do to her, all the pleasure they could bring her.

Life had been only waiting in the wings until that moment he'd first touched her, and turned her from a rather shy, coolly controlled girl into a warm and passionate woman.

Remembering how it had been, she felt heat and a shameful desire flood through her body.

As though her erotic thoughts had attracted his attention, he glanced up.

Under his gaze she felt her nipples grow firm beneath the thin satin of her nightdress. Colour pouring into her face, she folded her arms defensively across her chest.

He laughed softly. 'The old chemistry's still there, I see.'

'Don't flatter yourself,' she snapped. 'I was thinking of Gerald.'

Suddenly he was standing over her. 'Were you really?' His hands cupping her elbows, he lifted her to her feet and slowly and deliberately pulled her to him.

The little hairs at the nape of her neck stood on end, and all the strength drained from her legs, leaving them like jelly as she felt the muscular firmness of his body.

'Let me go,' she croaked.

Without a word he took advantage of her parted lips and began to kiss her, coaxingly at first, then demandingly, deepening the kiss until her head was spinning and her entire being was crying out for more.

Though she tried desperately to remain cool and in control, within seconds she was a quivering wreck, lost and mindless.

When he eased her nightdress from her shoulders and let it fall in a satin puddle at her feet she was incapable of protest.

His mouth at her breast sent something like an electric shock running through her, and she gave a shuddering gasp.

While he suckled sweetly her breathing grew faster and uneven, her heart raced wildly, and a pool of liquid heat formed in the pit of her stomach.

Eyes closed, she was making soft little sounds deep in her throat, her whole being concentrated on what he was doing to her, when abruptly he straightened. A second later his arms dropped to his sides and she was free.

Blind and dazed, she staggered, and would have fallen if he hadn't reached out and steadied her. He held her for a moment or two while she found her footing, then stepped back once more.

Her world turned upside down, her pride in tatters, she fought to pull herself together, to try and hide just how shattered she was.

Conscious that he was watching her, with a cruel little smile playing round his lips, and becoming aware of her nakedness, she blushed scarlet and fumbled to pick up and struggle into her nightdress.

'Isn't it a bit late for a display of maidenly modesty?' he mocked.

'Why did you…?' She faltered to a halt.

'I was merely proving to my own satisfaction that the chemistry *is* still there.'

'You're a brute and a beast and a devil—and I hate you!' she cried hoarsely.

'You may hate me, but you would still have gone to bed with me.'

Unable to deny it, she turned and fled in disarray.

Lying in bed, tense and frustrated, she tried to sort out the chaos of her thoughts and feelings.

What David had said was true. Though she no longer loved him, he still had such a hold over her senses that if he hadn't called a halt she *would* have gone to bed with him—in spite of everything.

Gerald's kisses, whilst pleasantly exciting, had never stirred her in this way. She had found it easy to resist him, easy to stay cool and virtually unmoved. In charge of her own emotions.

Perhaps *that* was why she had agreed to marry him. Though she found him attractive, he would never mean the world to her—which meant he would never be able to hurt her, as David had.

The realisation shook her.

How could she marry Gerald if he meant so little to her? It wouldn't be fair to him. A wife should love her husband wholeheartedly.

But if she cancelled the wedding at this late stage it would hurt both Gerald and his family, and she didn't want to hurt anyone.

Perhaps the best option would be to tell him the truth. Then, if he still wanted her, she would go ahead and marry him, and do her utmost to make him a good wife.

Recalling clearly how he'd said, *I miss you. Please come home soon*, she knew he must love her—or at least as much as he was capable of loving anyone other than himself…

While she recognised the truth of that last thought, she was shocked by her own disloyalty.

She was extremely lucky to have a fiancé like Gerald, she told herself sternly. Plenty of women would envy her and willingly take her place, without even looking for his faults.

And, when all was said and done, Gerald's faults were minor compared to the kind of blatant betrayal she had experienced at David's hands…

Dawn was lightening the sky before she finally fell into a restless doze, and it seemed as if she had barely closed her eyes when the alarm clock began to chirp merrily.

Dazed by lack of sleep, and feeling slightly nauseous, she struggled out of bed and made her way to the bathroom.

A hot shower revived her somewhat, and, eager to be gone, she put on a navy blue silk suit and swiftly arranged her hair into a neat coil.

When she was ready, and the rest of her things were packed, she picked up her flight bag and case and, with her soft handbag slung over one shoulder, hurried down the stairs.

It was barely six-thirty, and the old house was still and silent as she phoned for a taxi.

Having been assured that one would be with her in five minutes, she left her belongings in the hall and went through to the kitchen to make herself a cup of instant coffee while she listened for the doorbell.

Her coffee finished, she glanced at her watch. Almost ten minutes had passed and there was still no sign of the taxi.

'Good morning,' David's voice said.

Deborah hadn't heard him coming. She jumped a mile and spun round.

'Sorry if I startled you,' he added mendaciously.

Freshly showered and shaved, and dressed in smart casuals, he was lounging in the doorway.

Studying the faint smudges under her eyes, he remarked, 'You're looking very tired. Frustration keep you awake?'

Feeling the hot colour pour into her cheeks, she asked sharply, 'What do you want?'

His white smile was mocking. 'I thought a cup of coffee might be nice—if you'd care to make me one?'

'I wouldn't. I'm waiting for a taxi.'

Strolling over to spoon coffee into a cup and reheat the kettle, he told her, 'I'm afraid you're wasting your time.'

'What do you mean, I'm wasting my time?' she demanded.

'It won't be coming,' he said calmly. 'I pressed the redial button and cancelled it.'

'What on earth did you do that for?' Then, furiously, 'You had no right to cancel it! I have to get to the airport.'

Pouring boiling water into the cup, he assured her, 'As soon as I've finished my coffee I'll be happy to take you.'

'I don't want you to take me.'

He gave a theatrical sigh. 'How can you trample on my feelings like this? It shows a complete lack of—'

'Save your breath,' she told him curtly. 'I intend to go by taxi.'

'That could prove to be a mistake. Now, if you take my advice—'

Only too aware that he was enjoying baiting her, she cried, 'Will you please mind your own business?' and stormed out of the kitchen.

Reaching the hall, and finding herself alone, she breathed a sigh of relief. She had half expected him to either prevent her leaving or follow her.

She had stretched out a hand to pick up the receiver before she realised that her luggage and handbag were no longer where she'd left them.

Her hand dropped to her side and a little chill ran through her. It had to be David. But what was he up to? What was he hoping to achieve?

Her heart thudding hard against her ribs, she hurried back to the kitchen, where he was calmly drinking his coffee.

With what restraint she could muster, she asked, 'Perhaps you wouldn't mind telling me what you've done with my belongings?'

He emptied his cup before answering. 'They're in the boot of my car.'

'Well, you can just take them out again.'

He made no move, merely stood and looked at her.

'If *you* won't take them out *I* will.'

As she turned on her heel he informed her mildly, 'The car's locked.'

If it had just been her case and bag she would have gone without them. But her passport was in her handbag and she needed it to travel.

Losing any remaining cool, she cried, 'Will you get it into your head that I've no intention of letting you drive me to the airport?'

'Would you prefer to cancel your flight?'

'No, I *wouldn't* prefer to cancel my flight.'

'Then I'm ready to start when you are.'

She clenched her hands in vexation. Why was he being so stubborn about it? It made no sense.

'Just tell me *why* you're so determined to take me.'

Blue eyes gleaming, he said, 'Perhaps I want a chance to kiss you goodbye.'

'You could—' She broke off abruptly.

'Kiss you goodbye here?' He finished her sentence with a wicked smile.

'No, I—'

'You suggested it.'

Before she could make any protest his arms had gone round her and he was kissing her with a shocking expertise that left her limp and quivering.

It was a little while before she could summon up enough will-power to pull herself free.

Trying to hide how shaken she was, she managed, 'Now you've kissed me goodbye, perhaps you'd be kind enough to give me back my things?'

He shook his head. 'You can't call that a proper goodbye kiss. That was just getting into practice for the real thing.'

'Why are you doing this?' she asked jerkily.

'Let's just say I have my reasons. Shall we go?' Turning on his heel, he led the way.

Seething with impotent fury, she perforce followed him into the hall and out of the front door.

It was a lovely spring day. The sun shone, thin and bright as a sheet of beaten gold, birds sang joyously, and the air was cool and sparkling.

'Isn't it a beautiful morning?' he remarked cheerfully as he opened the car door for her.

She was about to get in without deigning to reply when some premonition, some sixth sense, set a warning bell jangling, and she hesitated.

'Forgotten something?' he enquired.

Playing for time, she said, 'I promised I'd ring Gerald and let him know which flight I'm on.'

'It will be the middle of the night in New York,' he pointed out. 'And if you're only going to leave a message it would make more sense to do it at the airport. Traffic will soon be starting to build up, so we can't afford to waste too much time…'

His attitude was so prosaic, so down-to-earth, that, realising she was just being foolish, she got in and proceeded to fasten her seatbelt.

He slid in beside her, turned on the engine, and a few seconds later they were leaving Thornton Court behind them.

As they made their way out of London, in the relative quiet of early morning, she was lulled by the movement of the car. Her eyes gradually closed.

She was floating on cloud nine, dreaming that David—the David of old—was kissing her, when, his lips brushing hers, he whispered, 'Wake up, Sleeping Beauty. We're here.'

As her heavy lids lifted he kissed her again, softly, sweetly. Wanting that kiss to go on, she closed them once more, but he took her hand and urged her from the car.

Stumbling out, still half-asleep, she found they were parked not at a busy airport terminal, but outside an old Elizabethan manor house.

Rothlands.

She gaped at it speechlessly.

It conjured up far too many memories. Memories that were almost too poignant to bear. Memories that were best forgotten.

The last time she had seen Rothlands the rotting door had been hanging loose on its hinges, panes of glass had been missing from the mullioned windows, part of the roof had caved in, and ivy had been rampaging everywhere.

Now it was in good order. Its roof had been rebuilt with genuine old slates, the ruined door replaced by one made of solid oak, its leaded windows restored with beautiful old glass and the ivy trimmed back.

After their breakup—though she had never asked and no one had ever mentioned it—she had expected him to have put the house back on the market.

Clearly she had been wrong.

Finding her voice, she demanded, 'Why have you brought me here?'

'I thought you might be interested.' Producing a large ornate key, he unlocked the door. 'Come and see the inside.'

It was the last thing she wanted to do.

Apart from any other consideration, the thought that she had once hoped to be mistress of this lovely old place was too painful.

Standing her ground, she said thickly, 'No, thank you. I don't want to see the inside.'

Before she could catch her breath, however, she found herself gently but firmly propelled into the large hall, now with polished floorboards, panelled walls, and a handsome oak staircase.

As the door closed behind them she struggled to free herself. 'Will you stop manhandling me? I don't know what you think you're going to achieve, but I—'

'Come and have some breakfast and I'll tell you.'

'I don't want any breakfast. I've a plane to catch.' Then, trying to quell her growing feeling of alarm, she said boldly, 'I insist that you take me to the airport.'

He shook his head regretfully. 'I'm afraid you're not in a position to insist on anything. You see, I hold the whip hand.'

A chill ran down her spine. 'I don't know what you're talking about.'

'As soon as we've had breakfast I'll make everything clear.'

'I don't want any breakfast,' she repeated.

'I'm sure I can change your mind. The kitchen's this way.' He walked across the hall and disappeared through a door at the end.

Damn him! she thought violently. She *wouldn't* be dictated to. Turning on her heel, she pulled open the heavy front door and ran to the car.

It was securely locked.

She ground her teeth. No wonder he'd been so laid-back about walking away and leaving her. He must have anticipated her move and be smiling to himself.

For a moment or two she debated making a run for it. But where was there to run to?

Pityme, the only place she could hope to get a taxi, was a good mile away. And, even if she could get there without him stopping her, her handbag and passport were still in the car boot.

With a feeling of helplessness she admitted defeat. It seemed he *did* hold the whip hand. At least for the time being.

It was cold comfort to find the front door still standing ajar. She didn't want to give him a laugh by having to ring the bell.

Bracing herself, she made her way inside and crossed the hall. At the kitchen door she paused. Common sense told her it was no use being angry. She would have to co-operate—at least to the point of hearing what he had to say.

Once she knew what his motives were for bringing her here, she might be able to get him to see sense. Then, hopefully, she could catch a later flight.

Taking a deep breath, she opened the door into a kitchen

that was large and sunny, with white walls, black beams, and comfortable-looking furniture.

Gerald had once told her he wouldn't be seen dead in a kitchen, whereas David, looking quite at home, was standing by an electric cooker frying rashers of bacon in a business-like manner.

She was amazed that someone so masculine should appear completely at ease in what she'd always regarded as a feminine domain. Though of course, she reminded herself, many chefs were men.

Glancing over his shoulder, he asked, 'Bacon and eggs do?'

'I'm not hungry.'

The delicious smell of frying bacon caused her mouth to water, making nonsense of the claim.

Unruffled, he said, 'Well, *I* am. And I don't fancy eating alone.'

Indicating a chintz-covered armchair in front of the inglenook fireplace, he suggested, 'Why not make yourself at home while I finish cooking?'

'I'd like to ring Gerald.'

'It's too early.'

'I'll leave a message.'

'You can ring him in a while…when you know for sure what you want to say.'

'But I—'

'Later.'

Seeing she wasn't going to budge him, she sat down reluctantly, memories of their first visit to Rothlands crowding in. Memories that were bittersweet, that tugged at her heartstrings. Memories of the eager girl she had been, and how, as she and David had walked hand in hand through the ruined rooms, she had envisaged just how beautiful they could be.

She had imagined David and herself living here, the old

place filled with love and laughter and happiness. Imagined blazing log fires in the winter, tea on the lawn in summer, a fat little pony in the stables, their children learning to ride…

Now, remembering all the love and dreams for the future they had shared, a tremor ran through her.

Proving he missed very little, David said, 'I haven't had time to light the fire, but if you're not warm enough I'll turn up the central heating.'

'I'm plenty warm enough, thank you.'

He studied her, his blue eyes speculative, and, pinned by that steady gaze, Deborah wished she had said she was cold.

When he'd returned his attention to the frying pan she looked around the pleasant room, with its air of simplicity and serenity.

Sunshine painted lozenges of light across the smoothly flagged floor, and made softly moving patterns of lilac leaves on the opposite wall.

She had always considered that the kitchen was the heart of any house, and at one time she had hoped to design *this* kitchen herself.

But whoever *had* finally designed it had done a good job, she was forced to concede. She could find no fault with it. Though it boasted all mod cons, somehow it still managed to give the impression of being in period.

The mullioned windows, set either side of a central oak door, looked out over a paved terrace and a smooth stretch of lawn. Beyond that was a stand of mature trees, and over to the right what appeared to be kitchen gardens with some glasshouses.

'I take it you're living at Rothlands now?' She spoke the thought aloud.

Putting plates to warm, and cutlery on the oak table, he said, 'Yes. Getting the old place put to rights took a long time, but I finally sold my flat and moved in about three months ago.'

Without intending to, she found herself asking, 'On your own?'

'No.'

'Oh.' Shaken to the core by his answer—the fact that another woman was living in *her* house—Deborah swallowed hard. But what had she expected? That he would live alone for the rest of his life?

He raised a dark brow. 'You seem surprised.'

'The house *feels* empty.' She said the first thing that came into her head.

'Sarah is away, visiting her mother.'

So he was married. Her heart felt as though it was being constricted by strands of barbed wire.

But why should it matter to her whether he was married or not? She might be getting married herself.

When she was sure her voice was steady enough, she asked, as casually as possible, 'So you have a wife?'

'No.'

Though it made precious little difference whether it was a long-term relationship or marriage, she was ridiculously relieved.

'What do you think of the kitchen?' He changed the subject smoothly. 'If my memory serves me correctly, you intended to plan it yourself?'

His words were like stones thrown at her.

When, routed, she said nothing, he took warm rolls from the oven and poured boiling water into the cafetière before pressing, 'Does the finished result meet with your approval?'

'It's wonderful.' She did her best to keep her voice level.

'Sarah loves it.'

'Did she…design it?'

'No.' He began to dish up the meal. 'As a matter of fact I did.'

'*You* did?'

'Though I may not rate as a designer, I know what I want and how to achieve it.'

There was a strange nuance to the apparently innocuous words, but before she could try to fathom it he said, 'Come and eat.'

When he pulled out a chair for her she sat down without further protest, though her appetite had totally vanished.

Having put a generous helping of bacon and eggs in front of her, he sat down opposite and offered her the basket of crisp rolls.

'I'm afraid the rolls are out of the freezer,' he told her cheerfully. 'But I haven't been home since Paul's accident. It was more convenient to pack a case and stay at Thornton—especially with Sarah being away.'

Every mention of Sarah tightened the barbed wire around her heart.

Deborah picked up her knife and fork and began to eat. The meal was nicely cooked and tasty, but it might have been ashes in her mouth.

When both their plates were empty, he put them in the dishwasher and poured the coffee.

Gathering herself, she began, 'You wanted me to have breakfast, and now I've had breakfast—'

'Did you enjoy it?'

'Yes, thank you,' she said politely. Then, refusing to be sidetracked, 'So now perhaps you'll be good enough to tell me why you made me miss my plane?'

'Two reasons. I wanted you to see Rothlands, and I needed a chance to talk to you.'

'Well, I'm here, so will you please get on and say what you have to say? That way I can hopefully catch a later flight.'

He shook his head.

Alarm bells ringing, she insisted, 'I have to go back today. If...if everything's all right, I'm getting married tomorrow. And you can't stop me,' she added defiantly.

'Do you know, I rather think I can?'

'If you imagine you can keep me here against my will, you're quite mistaken.'

'I don't believe I am mistaken. After all, no one knows where you are. Everyone will believe you've gone back to the States, and—'

'Gerald is sure to phone to see where I am.'

'Not if I ring him first and tell him you've decided not to go back. It's my guess that hurt pride will prevent him pursuing the matter...'

His voice dropping to a menacing whisper, he went on, 'When the builders were working on this place they discovered some old cellars. So I could keep you a prisoner here for as long as it suits me.'

Unsteadily, she accused, 'Now you're just trying to scare me.'

The laughter lines around his eyes deepened and his face relaxed into a smile. 'I'm succeeding too, judging by your expression.'

Crossly, she said, 'I wish you'd stop playing games and tell me exactly what you want.'

His smile disappeared.

'You.'

CHAPTER SIX

'WHAT?'

'Surely it's simple enough? I want you, and I intend to have you.'

Convinced he was still playing games, she asked, 'Won't Sarah kick up a fuss?'

He shook his head. 'I doubt if it'll bother Sarah. She's very broad-minded.'

'So you're planning a cosy little *ménage à trois*? Well, I'm sorry, but three in a bed isn't my style.'

'Nor mine.'

'So Sarah and I will be allotted alternate nights?'

'There's no need for jealousy. You can warm my bed *every* night if you want to.'

Gritting her teeth, she asked, 'Then Sarah isn't the jealous type?'

'Not that I know of. Of course she might prove to be, if her husband decided to take a walk on the wild side. But as Tom's turned sixty, and his only interest is gardening, I think it's unlikely.'

Feeling like a non-swimmer who had mistakenly jumped into the deep end and just been rescued, Deborah said, 'So Sarah's your housekeeper?'

'Correct.'

'Why did you say she was your girlfriend?'

'I didn't. You jumped to that conclusion.'

But he'd let her go on believing it.

'Now there's no jealous rival,' he continued, 'do you feel any happier about moving in with me?'

'No, I don't.'

'Well, if you're not happy, at least I'll make sure you're satisfied.'

'I wish you'd be serious.'

'I'm deadly serious.'

Seeing the steely look in his eyes, and suddenly realising he meant every word, she stammered, 'Y-you must be stark staring mad.'

'Not quite. Though I did go a little crazy when you walked out on me. Making you pay for that has become something of an obsession. An obsession that I need to tackle before it *does* send me crazy…'

He had always acted as though he was the innocent party, she thought resentfully. As though he had no need to feel guilty at all.

At times she wished she had brought his perfidy into the open and faced him with it, but a perverse kind of pride had kept her silent.

When she had told him she'd made a mistake, that her career was more important to her than marriage, she had seen the look of devastation on his face and felt convinced that he still loved her.

But if he'd loved her enough he wouldn't have had a fling with her best friend.

No, *more* than a fling.

If it had been just a fling, with no serious consequences, she might have forgiven him.

But, as it was, a child had been conceived—and you didn't get much more serious than that.

'When I walked out on you, I had a good reason.'

'I didn't much like coming a very poor second to your career.'

'It wasn't—' She broke off abruptly.

His gaze sharpened. 'Wasn't your career?'

It was too late now to take any other path, and at least while he thought she'd ended things because of her career it saved her pride. And, out of everything she'd once had, pride was all that was left.

She shook her head. 'I was going to say it wasn't an easy decision to make.'

'Whereas my decision to seek some recompense was.'

'But you've done nothing for three years. I don't understand why you've made a move now.'

'Circumstances—something I was told, and the fact that you were about to marry someone else—brought things to a head. I want you back.'

Her heart seemed to stop. 'I won't marry you.'

'I wasn't asking you to. I'm no longer interested in marriage. I just want you to be there and available whenever I want you.'

The casual contempt behind the proposition stung like a whiplash.

Hoarsely, she said, 'I won't be your mistress.'

'From now on you'll be anything I want you to be,' he stated.

'I will *not*!'

His face was like granite. 'You will if you care about Paul and your family.'

'I don't understand,' she said blankly.

'Then I'll spell it out for you. Paul's in deep financial trouble and has been forced to borrow heavily. It's only my backing that's still keeping him afloat.'

'He can't be in as deeply as you're trying to make out. The company's still functioning.'

'Only with my support.'

'If Paul was really desperate he could always mortgage Thornton Court.'

'By the time Kathy asked me for help Thornton Court was already mortgaged up to the hilt. When they found they were unable to keep up the repayments I stepped in and bought the place.'

'So *you* own Thornton Court.'

'That's right.'

She stared at him, aghast.

'Now, there are two alternatives,' he went on, his voice dispassionate. 'If you agree to do as I want, I'll wipe the slate clean and make Paul his own master again...'

'And if I don't?' whispered Deborah.

'I'm prepared to withdraw my support and let Hartleys crash.'

As she half shook her head, he said, 'Believe me, it would be easy. Inside information suggests that Crofts have been buying every one of the company's shares they can get their hands on. If you remember, I mentioned a big foreign contract, waiting to be signed? Should I fail to sign, the deal will fall through and share prices will tumble like a house of cards. If there is panic selling, it will enable Crofts to snap up all the shares they need to get a controlling interest.'

White to the lips, she said, 'You wouldn't do that...for Kathy's sake.'

'Don't be too sure.'

'Could you live with what they'd all think of you?'

He smiled with cynical self-mockery. 'Everyone knows how hard I've worked to try and save the company. No one would blame me if I failed.'

'I could tell them what you've just told me.'

'You *could*—but if I denied it, who would they believe? The family could well be split. In any case, the damage would be done.'

There was silence apart from the homely ticking of a grandmother clock. Aware that his eyes were fixed on her face, Deborah struggled to take in all the implications.

After a moment, she burst out, 'This is nothing but coercion! A form of blackmail...'

'Try to think of it as friendly persuasion.'

'What about Gerald?' she asked desperately.

'If he's still interested, he can have you back when I've finished with you.'

Recoiling from his contemptuous words, she managed, 'When will that be?'

'As soon as I've finally got you out of my system.'

'You're warped and twisted.'

'If I am, it's what you've made me.'

She bit her lip until she tasted blood. It seemed their ill-starred relationship had damaged them both.

'And it's not as bad as it might be,' David went on ironically. 'After all, I'm giving you a choice.'

'How generous of you.'

Unmoved by her sarcasm, he went on, 'Should you choose to leave, I'll arrange to have my jet fly you back to the States as soon as possible. If you choose to stay, all you have to do is ring Delcy and tell him the wedding's off.'

If she just cancelled the wedding out of hand Gerald was bound to be hurt and furious. It would mean the end of her career with Delcy Fashion House.

And worse. He—or at least his family—wielded quite a lot of power in the world of fashion, so it would probably mean the end of her career, full stop.

She would have nothing left.

'I can't simply cancel the wedding,' she cried.

As though reading her thoughts, David said, 'I refuse to believe you really love a man like Delcy, so I presume it's because of your career?'

She flushed scarlet.

'Just as I thought.' He smiled with grim humour. 'Well, if your career means more to you than your brother and family, it shouldn't be too hard a decision to make.' Briskly, he added, 'Now, you have five minutes to choose which option you want to go with.'

While the minutes ticked slowly past she thought through everything he'd just said. She had little doubt that he *could* do as he'd threatened, but she didn't believe for an instant that he would.

Surely the old David she had known and loved would never betray his brother-in-law and ruin his sister's happiness? Nor would he force any woman to be his mistress against her will.

Only he was no longer the old David. He was a different man. A man capable of being hard and cruel, capable of destroying other people's lives to get what he wanted.

Quite capable.

But would he do it?

This new David was an unknown quantity…

'Well, have you decided? The foreign contract has to be signed by noon. If it isn't, and the news gets into the papers…' He didn't finish the sentence. But then he didn't need to.

Worrying at her lower lip, she wondered if she should call his bluff.

If he was bluffing…

But suppose he wasn't? Could she afford to risk it?

The answer was no, and she knew it.

Her blood seemed to turn to ice in her veins. How would she bear sleeping with a man who hated her? Who only wanted revenge?

When she had believed that they loved each other making love with him had been blissful, rapturous, as close to heaven as anyone but an angel could get.

To be forced into it now would be unbearable, the worst kind of humiliation. But perhaps he didn't mean to go through with it? Maybe he would be satisfied just to break up her wedding plans and scare her?

Dared she chance it?

Had she any alternative?

If Paul lost the company he'd worked so hard for she

would never forgive herself. It would haunt her for the rest of her life.

Making up her mind, she said, 'Very well, I'll stay,' and was pleased to find that her voice was even, under control.

His face impassive, he said, 'I'm delighted you've seen sense.'

Reaching across the table, he took her left hand, and before she'd realised his intention he had slipped off her engagement ring. 'You won't be needing to wear this any longer.'

'What do you intend to do with it?'

He dropped it into his pocket. 'When I send someone over to New York to collect the rest of your belongings I'll make sure Delcy gets it back. Now, as it's still too early to call him, would you like to see the rest of the house before I bring in your case?'

It was a bittersweet prospect, and she hesitated for a moment or two before rising to her feet and following him in silence.

All the work on the interior had been done with the same sympathetic care as the exterior, and the old house was as serenely beautiful as she'd once imagined it.

It made her eyes burn with unshed tears when she thought of what might have been.

But it was no use thinking like that, she told herself fiercely. Neither the house nor the happiness she had once envisaged would ever be hers, so it was no use repining.

The dining-room, the library and the morning-room were furnished with what appeared to be genuine period pieces. In the instances where the twenty-first century was in evidence it failed to detract from the charm.

Only David's study-cum-office was blatantly modern, with a businesslike desk and a state-of-the-art computer and communications system.

The living-room, to the right of the hall, ran across the

end of the house. Once again it was furnished with lovingly polished antiques, while a contemporary suite in soft, natural leather and a television and music centre somehow blended in to the whole without looking out of place.

'Perhaps you consider it to be under-furnished?' David queried, as she looked around.

'No.'

'You don't feel it needs a woman's touch?' he pursued sardonically.

'If you mean frills and flounces and ornaments, not at all,' she informed him shortly. 'I think it's perfect as it is.'

'It's pleasant,' he agreed. 'With windows on three walls, and lying east-west, it gets the sun for most of the day. As does our bedroom.'

The softly spoken rider made her stomach clench.

As though he knew, he smiled, before inviting, 'Come and see what you think of the upstairs.'

They returned to the hall, and, looking at the perfectly proportioned minstrels' gallery that had been lovingly restored, Deborah could see why it had taken so long to put the house to rights.

At the top of the stairs David turned left, and opening doors on either side of the main corridor, remarked, 'Careful planning has given all the rooms their own *en suite* facilities, but as you can see they're not yet ready to receive guests.'

All the rooms had black beams, oak floorboards, and their original fireplaces. All were delightful and full of character, but none of them was furnished.

Her heart dropped like a stone.

In spite of all David had said, she'd been clinging to the hope that he might not mean to carry things through—that he might let her have her own room.

Now she could see she'd been sadly mistaken.

Retracing his steps, he threw open a door to the right of the stairs. 'Not even the master bedroom is completely finished.' With a glint in his eye, he added, 'Though I'm sure you'll be pleased to know it does have a bed.'

Aware that he was watching her, waiting for a response, she bit her lip and said nothing.

The master bedroom, like the living-room, ran the width of the house. It was white-walled and simple, with a huge stone fireplace, a massive wardrobe, an old Spanish chest, two matching bow-fronted chests of drawers, and an imposing four-poster, complete with a faded crimson canopy.

Wrought-iron bedside lamps matched a central hanging lamp, and off-white rugs lay on the wide black floorboards.

In contrast, there was a large and frankly luxurious *en suite* bath and shower room, its fittings in ivory, the tiles flushed with the palest of pearly pinks.

'Not what you'd call particularly masculine,' he said, a shade ruefully, 'but both Kathy and Laura insisted that the tiles should be dawn-pink.'

Deborah felt a constriction in her chest.

A week or so before the breakup the three women had been looking through catalogues and discussing colour schemes for the various bathrooms. Though not usually a pink person, Deborah had picked dawn-pink as the one she liked for the master bedroom's *en suite* bathroom.

'Something wrong?' David queried, as they returned to the bedroom.

'No… No… I was just wondering where your housekeeper lives.'

Opening a couple of the casement windows to let in the sweet spring air, he told her, 'Sarah and her husband Tom, who, as I mentioned, incidentally takes care of the garden, have a flat over the old stables. When they were rebuilt I had one block converted into comfortable living quarters. Now, as you've seen all there is to see, and though it's still a bit on the early side, it might be as well to ring Delcy.'

Her common sense insisting that it was better to get it over with, she nodded.

When they were back in his study, David asked, 'Would you like me to talk to him?'

'No, I'd better.' Though she was dreading it, there was no way she could let Gerald hear the news from anyone but herself.

Making an effort to stay calm, she tapped in the number and waited.

After a few seconds she heard the rattle as someone fumbled to lift the receiver, then Gerald's irate voice demanding, 'Have you any idea what time it is?'

'I'm sorry, but I—'

'Darling!' he exclaimed. 'I should have realised it would be you. Which flight are you on? I'll do my best to meet you.'

'I'm not coming back,' she blurted out.

'You mean today?'

'I mean at all.'

There was a stunned silence, then he said, 'What about the wedding?'

'I can't marry you.'

'Don't be ridiculous, Deborah, you can't cancel the wedding at this late stage just because I didn't tell you about—'

'That isn't the reason.'

'What else could it possibly be? You were quite happy to marry me before the accident.'

Only too aware that David was listening to every word, she said, 'I know, but I've done a lot of thinking since, and I...I believe our marriage would be a mistake.'

'Look, you've obviously been under a lot of stress lately, and I—'

'It's not just that,' she broke in. 'I've realised I simply don't love you enough. It wouldn't be fair to marry you.'

'For God's sake, Deborah, you can't back out now. Apart from the financial aspect, it would make me look a complete fool…'

'I'm sorry, Gerald. Truly sorry. I never meant to hurt you.'

'If you do this to me you're finished as far as your career goes. I'll make sure that you never again work in the fashion industry.'

'Very well,' she said quietly. 'If it'll make you feel any better.'

'I don't believe this!' he burst out furiously. 'Have you gone mad? Or has that damned family of yours managed to influence you? It was obvious that none of them liked me. Well, if you won't tell me what's going on, I'll come over on the next plane and find out for myself.'

Panic-stricken, she begged, 'Please don't, Gerald. You'll only be wasting your time.'

'I'm determined to know why you're suddenly willing to throw everything away. There must be something you're not telling me. Some reason—'

In desperation, she admitted, 'There is… I've never told you this, but before I met you I was engaged to someone else. After a few months I broke it off…' She swallowed. 'It was David, my ex-fiancé, who came to New York to fetch me, and I… We…found the attraction was still there.'

'So that's why you went rushing off without a word, and why you've kept me at arm's length all this time. You're still in love with him! Well, if you think you can get away with dumping me and keeping my ring, you've got another think coming, you two-timing little—'

The receiver was taken from her nerveless fingers.

'That's quite enough, Delcy.' David's voice, though quiet, cracked like a whip. 'It's no use blaming Deborah. She didn't want to cancel the wedding at such short notice, but I insisted.'

'Who the hell are you?' Gerald snarled.

'I'm David Westlake. I spoke to you when I rang to advise Deborah of Paul's accident. Within a day or two I'll be sending someone over to New York to collect Deborah's things. I'll make sure you get your ring back safely. In addition, if you let me know how much you're out of pocket over the wedding arrangements, I'll be happy to write you a cheque.'

'It won't come cheap,' Gerald snapped maliciously.

'That isn't a problem.'

'Well, for your sake I hope you can get more out of the deceitful little jade than I ever got.'

His eyes meeting and holding Deborah's, David said silkily, 'I fully intend to.'

The threat sent a shiver down her spine.

Replacing the receiver, he asked, 'Do you want to tell your mother and Kathy about the change of plan, or shall I?'

Though she knew they would both be delighted, what would she say to them? How could she convincingly explain this sudden *volte-face*?

'I—I don't know what to say to them.'

'Keep it simple. Just say that rather than returning to the States you're moving in with me.'

Fraught and unhappy, dangerously close to tears, she said, 'You tell them.'

'Very well. I'll talk to them later.'

His blue eyes studying her pale face, he observed, 'You look absolutely all in. Why not go and lie down for a while? I'll bring your things up.'

Like a zombie, she made her way upstairs and into the master bedroom. It was pleasantly cool, and the air drifting in through the open windows carried the fragrance of early wallflowers.

Bone weary, she took off her suit and slip, and was about

to climb into the big four-poster when, asserting his right to walk in without knocking, David came in carrying her belongings.

Putting them down on the chest, he said, 'Jump into bed and I'll tuck you in.'

With a feeling of reprieve, she obeyed. She had been scared stiff that he wouldn't wait to try and claim the spoils of victory.

Walking into her mind as casually as he'd walked into the bedroom, he said, 'There's nothing I'd like better than to join you, but if I did I might not be able to tear myself away, and I have to go into the office for an hour…'

She breathed a sigh of relief. If he *had* joined her, she would have been in no state to fight back—shattered physically and mentally. And, while she might have been forced to agree to his terms, she had no intention of giving in without a struggle. No intention of making things easy for him.

'However…' He sat down on the edge of the bed. 'I've time for a quick kiss before I go.'

She stared up at him, her green eyes too big in her delicate, heart-shaped face.

His tone caustic, he remarked, 'There's really no need to look quite so scared. Anyone would think I had inch-long fangs and a taste for blood.'

'Being kissed by Dracula would be preferable,' she said thickly.

Laughing, he trailed a finger down the side of her neck. 'You certainly have the throat for it.'

'And, while you might not have fangs, you've certainly got a taste for blood.'

'I like a woman with spirit,' he said, and, grinning evilly, twirled an imaginary moustache. 'Taming you, my proud beauty, will add greatly to my pleasure.'

Once she would have laughed. Now she was too tense to see the funny side.

Getting no response, he bent his dark head and kissed her lightly.

With an effort of will she kept her eyes open and her mouth tightly closed, even when he used his tongue-tip to coax and tantalise.

Giving up momentarily, he traced the pure line of her jaw, making little shivers run through her and turning her skin to goose-flesh.

He felt those shivers and, his lips brushing her ear, ordered, 'Open your mouth for me.'

Ignoring the softly spoken command, she kept her lips pressed together.

All at once his teeth gave her earlobe a sharp, unexpected nip.

As she gasped in outrage his mouth closed over hers and plundered it ruthlessly, wreaking havoc, setting her heart pounding and her senses whirling.

The stress factor was so great that her lungs refused to work properly, and when he finally lifted his head her eyes were closed and she was on the point of blacking out.

Rising to his feet, he said evenly, 'I'll call into the hospital on my way home. Unless they need me, I don't intend to stay, so I should be back in time for a late lunch. In the meantime, have a nice sleep.'

A moment later, through the pounding of blood in her ears and the sound of her own rapid breathing, she heard the door close quietly behind him.

So that was where fighting him got her, she thought shakily. Perhaps if she'd kept things light it wouldn't have happened. But her stubborn resistance had angered him, and he was so much stronger than she was. She couldn't hope to win.

Though what else could she do but fight? How could she meekly give in?

However, if that punitive kiss was anything to go by, perhaps she should stick with passive resistance? Otherwise what lay ahead would be unendurable.

But when the man she loved no longer loved her, it would be unendurable anyway.

The man she loved…

Though she'd known from the start that the physical attraction was still there, she had told herself that the love she'd once felt for him had died when she'd moved to New York and met Gerald.

But instead of dying it had merely been lying dormant, and seeing him again had brought it surging back to life.

But how *could* she still love him after the way he'd betrayed her?

Yet she did. Love him with every fibre of her being. While all he felt for her was hatred and lust, she thought hopelessly.

Lying dry-eyed, too empty to cry, she was engulfed by a tide of despair. Eventually, worn out physically and emotionally, she fell into a troubled sleep.

When she awoke, the sun was low in the sky, casting the long blue-black shadows of trees across a golden green carpet of lawn.

A glance at her watch confirmed that it was early evening. Some of the leaden weight of despair had lifted, and she felt refreshed and energised.

A shower refreshed her even more, and, though she looked pale and wan, she knew a careful touch of make-up would disguise the pallor. Somehow she had to face David without showing quite how vulnerable she was.

But perhaps she'd let him scare her too easily? Maybe he didn't really intend to go ahead and make her his mistress?

Despite his threats, she couldn't believe he would try to

force her. Certainly not in cold blood. So if she could stay calm and in control, exercise restraint and avoid any kind of confrontation that would infuriate or incite him, he was almost bound to be reasonable.

She clung to that thought while she dressed in an oatmeal skirt and a silky brown top. Then, having brushed her hair and taken it up into its usual shining coil, she made her way down the stairs, feeling almost confident.

After looking in both the living-room and his study, she found David in the kitchen.

Wearing casual trousers and a navy blue shirt, he was tossing a mixed salad in a large wooden bowl. Despite the teatowel draped round his lean hips he managed to appear overwhelmingly masculine.

He looked up and, his expression neutral, neither friendly nor unfriendly, asked, 'Feeling better?'

She tried for cheerfulness. 'Much better.'

'I'm pleased to hear it.' Blue eyes glinting, he added, 'I don't want you to be tired tonight.'

She changed colour, and her fleeting feeling of near-confidence abruptly drained away.

'Why don't you sit down?' he suggested as, intent on hiding her reaction to his veiled threat, she hovered, looking anywhere but at him.

The windows were open wide, letting in the mild evening air, while a log fire blazed in the huge grate, bringing the room to life.

She'd always loved an open fire, and just the sight of it was oddly comforting. Sitting down in one of the armchairs, she stared into the leaping flames.

He handed her a glass of pale sherry. 'I hope you still like it dry?'

'Yes, thank you.'

'Dinner will be ready in about ten minutes,' he went on.

'Seared salmon, new potatoes and salad, followed by fruit and cheese. As I'm no chef, I've kept it simple.'

'It sounds very nice,' she said politely.

'You must be hungry?'

She wasn't at all hungry, but, not wanting to rock the boat, she lied, 'A bit.'

'When I came up to see if you wanted any lunch you were sleeping like a baby, so I decided not to disturb you.'

The knowledge that he must have stood and watched her while she slept gave her an odd feeling.

When she said nothing, leaving the ball in her court, he went on with his preparations for the meal in silence.

For a while she sipped her sherry and watched his face—the sweep of dark lashes against his hard cheek as he looked down; his small frown of concentration as he turned the salmon fillets; the way his lips pursed as he whistled softly…

Glancing up, he caught her eye.

Reminding herself that she needed to keep things as amicable as possible, she asked, 'Did you get into the hospital?'

'Yes. They were pleased and relieved to hear that the South American deal was all signed and settled, and even more pleased to know that you won't be getting married after all. It seems that none of them really cared for Delcy.'

'Did you tell them—?' She broke off awkwardly.

'That you were here with me? Yes, I told them. They were delighted that you'd "seen sense at last",' he added dryly.

Her free hand curled into a fist, the nails digging into her palm. But, refusing to rise to the bait, she asked, 'How was Paul?'

Deftly dishing up salmon and potatoes, David said, 'Happy that we're together again. He's starting to look considerably better, and is already talking about when he's back on his feet… Ready to eat?'

As soon as she was seated in the chair he'd pulled out for her he helped her to salad before pouring them each a glass of white wine.

Then, taking a seat opposite, he raised his glass, and, his expression mocking, toasted, 'Here's to our new relationship.'

She looked at him in mutinous silence.

He clicked his tongue reprovingly. 'No response?'

If it was a response he wanted, he should have one. Smiling sweetly, she picked up her glass and threw the contents in his face.

CHAPTER SEVEN

IMMEDIATELY regretting her action, she watched in horror as the wine ran down his lean cheeks and dripped onto his shirt.

'I—I'm sorry,' she stammered. 'I shouldn't have done that.'

He wiped his face and throat with a table napkin. 'As I remarked earlier, I like a woman with spirit.'

Tossing the damp napkin aside, he leaned forward and refilled her glass, as though challenging her to repeat the action.

Refusing to pick up the gauntlet, she looked down at her plate, angry with herself for losing her temper. Where was the cool self-control, the restraint she'd resolved on?

As it was, she had left herself wide open to retaliation. Though to all intents and purposes he was taking it calmly, it didn't mean to say he wouldn't make her pay for it later.

She was quaking inwardly at the thought when he said, with studied casualness, 'Don't let your food get cold,' and picked up his own knife and fork.

Though her appetite was non-existent, she forced herself to follow suit. But, aware that his eyes were on her face, and unnerved by that steady regard, she ate automatically, without tasting a thing.

Apart from asking politely if she'd had enough, and offering her cheese and fruit, which she refused, he made no attempt at conversation—and she could think of nothing to say.

It was the most fraught meal of her life, and she'd brought it on herself. If things had stayed on a reasonably friendly footing it would have been so much easier, she thought regretfully.

When their coffee was finished he cleared away the dishes before suggesting, 'As it's such a pleasant evening, would you like to take a stroll?'

She was about to accept the olive branch, if that was what it was, when he added, 'You'll find the gardens have been transformed. Particularly the walled garden.'

Remembering what had happened in the walled garden the first time they'd seen it, she went hot all over. She was trying to think of some good reason to refuse when he added smoothly, 'Unless, of course, you'd prefer an early night?'

Caught between the devil and the deep blue sea, she chose what seemed to be the lesser of two evils. 'No, I'd like to go for a stroll, please.'

The corner of his long mouth twitched.

Realising that she'd sounded like a frightened adolescent, she flushed.

Indicating his wet shirt, he said, 'If you'll excuse me, I'd better get changed first.'

Unwilling to look back, afraid to look forward, she waited with an odd feeling of being suspended in time and space.

He returned quite quickly, looking disturbingly attractive in a fine indigo polo-necked sweater. Over his arm was her oatmeal jacket.

'Now the sun's going down it's turning a little cool. I thought you might need this.'

'Thank you.'

Having helped her into it, he closed the door behind them. The evening was calm, with not a breath of wind, and the blue air was heady with the scent of lilac.

They strolled through the carefully tended gardens without speaking or touching, but as they crossed the smoothly sloping lawns towards the walled garden he took her hand.

Just his touch made her tremble.

She wanted to withdraw it, but, afraid of a confrontation, left it where it was.

Hand in hand, in a parody of their former closeness, they made their way through a small wooden door in the tall, pink brick wall.

When they had last walked through it everything had been wild and overgrown, thick with nettles and brambles. The old stone fountain, its basin cracked, had been dry and full of leaves, and long summer grasses, heavy with seed heads and pollen, had taken over what had once been lawn.

Now everything was cared for—the paths clear, the lawn like green velvet, the borders bright with spring flowers and fragrant with herbs. Roses and wisteria, honeysuckle and Virginia creeper climbed the walls, and in the centre the fountain was throwing up a sparkling jet of water.

In her mind's eye the past was clearer than the present, and, seeing it as it had once been, she found herself struggling to hold back the memories. But in spite of all her efforts they besieged her, bittersweet and poignant…

Picking their way through the mass of vegetation, fingers entwined… Pausing from time to time to smile at each other and kiss… David spreading a picnic blanket amidst a sea of tall dried grasses, then slowly undressing her… The scent of late roses on the still air… The October sunshine gilding her slender limbs… His hands and his mouth roving over her sun-warmed flesh while he whispered how beautiful she was, how much he loved and wanted her…

Now all that love had turned to hate.

'Tom has done wonders, don't you think?' David's voice broke into her thoughts.

Her throat feeling dry and constricted, she answered, 'Yes, it's beautiful.'

Then, in an effort to keep the conversation going and stop her thoughts slipping back, 'I don't know how he's managed to achieve so much in three years.'

'Because he and Sarah lived in Pityme, he was able to start on the gardens even before work on the house got underway.'

'I'm surprised you decided to keep it.'

'Perhaps foolishly, I cherished the hope that you might come back to me, that you might really be the girl I'd thought you were.'

Hurt beyond endurance, she cried, 'I would never have left you if *you'd* really been the man I'd thought *you* were.'

As soon as the words were spoken she wished them unsaid.

He stopped in his tracks and, his hands gripping her upper arms, turned her towards him. 'What did I do to make you leave me? Tell me.'

What was the use? It was too late. What was done couldn't be undone, and nothing could be gained by telling him now.

'Perhaps it was because I suggested that we had a family when you have no time for children?' David said, watching her carefully.

'Of course I have time for children.'

'Are you expecting me to believe that you and Delcy hadn't ruled out having babies?'

'*I* hadn't.'

A sneer in his voice, he said, 'At least one to satisfy your biological urge? Brought up by a nanny so it wouldn't interfere too much with your precious *career*?'

She opened her mouth to say that as he'd rejected his own child he was a fine one to talk, but a fierce pride was making her unable to admit that she ever *knew* about his and Claire's illegitimate baby. She closed it again, leaving the damning indictment left unspoken.

'Isn't that how it would have been?' he pressed.

'It doesn't matter any longer,' she said wearily.

He frowned. 'So, tell me what you meant by, *I would*

never have left you if you'd really been the man I'd thought you were.'

'Maybe I just stopped looking at you through rose-coloured glasses.'

'I think you meant a good deal more than that.'

Her lips pressed together, a mulish look on her face, she stayed silent.

His fingers tightened on her upper arms, as if he meant to shake the truth out of her, but after a moment he sighed and let her go.

Even so, she could tell that her refusal to explain her remark had made him angry, and her heart sank.

This time he made no attempt to take her hand, and they walked on in silence until they reached the far end of the garden, before returning to the house in the gathering dusk.

The fire had died into whitish ash, and the kitchen was distinctly cool. Closing the windows, he queried, 'Would you like anything to drink?'

'No, thank you.'

She wished she'd said yes when, having bolted the door, he remarked, 'In that case we may as well go straight up.'

She moved like someone in a trance, unable to think or feel, and his hand rested lightly on the small of her back as he escorted her up the stairs.

When they reached the bedroom he steered her in and, closing the door behind them, switched on the lamps and helped her out of her jacket.

'Perhaps you'd like to use the bathroom first?'

Wondering how far he intended to carry things, she obeyed. There was no lock on the door. She creamed off her make-up and cleaned her teeth, but, unwilling to get undressed, went back to the bedroom without showering.

'All done?' he queried politely.

At her equally polite, 'Yes, thank you,' he disappeared into the bathroom, closing the door behind him.

A second or two later she heard the shower start.

Once again she found herself wishing she could run. But there was nowhere to run to.

He returned barefoot, wearing a short white towelling robe. Raising a dark level brow, he said, 'Still dressed, I see.'

When, her face set, she said nothing, he moved behind her, and before she could protest began to remove the pins from her coil of hair.

As it tumbled round her shoulders he remarked with satisfaction, 'That's better.'

She remembered with a pang that he'd always liked her hair loose or in a plait, rather than taken up.

Sliding a cool hand between her neck and the curtain of ash-blonde hair that cascaded down her back, he lifted the heavy, silken mass and let it ripple through his fingers.

'I've been looking forward to seeing your hair spread across my pillow.'

Jerking away, she spun round to face him. 'I don't want to sleep with you,' she said thickly. 'If you force me—'

'I wouldn't dream of forcing you.'

She was breathing a sigh of relief when he added softly, 'All I'll need to do is kiss you, touch you… As I proved the other night, the sexual chemistry's still there.'

Unable to deny it, she looked anywhere but at him.

'Why did you keep Delcy at arm's length?'

His sudden question took her by surprise.

When she failed to answer, he pursued, 'You're a passionate women, so you must have had a reason?'

She took a steadying breath. 'What makes you so sure I *did* keep him at arm's length?'

'If it wasn't the truth he wouldn't have been angry enough to admit it. After all, it doesn't reflect too well on his powers of seduction. So, why did you?' he pressed.

Unwilling to discuss it, she bit her lip.

'Wasn't he sexy enough to tempt you? Was marrying him merely a career move?'

Touched on the raw, she cried angrily, 'No, it wasn't! And, for your information, Gerald is not only blond and good-looking, but *extremely* sexy. Women throw themselves at him.'

'Really? So what held *you* back?'

Convinced that he was just amusing himself at her expense, she looked at him stonily.

An ironic gleam in his eye, he suggested, 'Possibly you thought if you gave your all too soon he might not marry you?'

'Or perhaps I've simply stopped trusting men.'

'If that's the case, there must be a reason,' he pointed out silkily. 'And I'd very much like to know what it is.'

It was almost as if he *wanted* her to challenge him, *wanted* her to bring into the open how he'd betrayed her trust. Well, she wouldn't allow him the satisfaction of trailing her pride in the dust.

'I'm not answering any more questions,' she flashed. 'And I wish you'd stop tormenting me. I'm not here for your entertainment.'

'Ah, now, that's where you're wrong. That's *exactly* what you're here for. So, if you're not willing to answer my questions, you can entertain me in some other way.'

Her mouth going dry, she said, 'What other way? What do you mean?'

Sitting down in the nearest chair, he stretched out his long bare legs and, crossing one ankle over the other, said with the air of a sultan addressing a slave girl, 'I mean you can strip for me.'

'What?'

'Take off your clothes.'

'I'll do no such thing!'

'You'll undress for me, and come to me.'

'I will *not*.'

'I think you will.'

No, she thought shakily, she couldn't stand here and take off her clothes while he sat and watched her in cold blood.

Her voice husky, she begged, 'Please, David…'

'What's the big deal? You've taken your clothes off for me in the past.'

'That was different,' she protested.

'In what way?'

'Then I…we…we loved each other,' she stammered.

'And now?'

'It's just lust.'

'You think there's a difference?' He raised a mocking eyebrow.

'Of course there's a difference.'

'Surely that depends.'

'On what?' she couldn't help asking.

'On what you *mean* by love. Caring sex? Companionship? An insurance against loneliness?'

'All those things, and much more.'

'Faithfulness?' he asked, almost casually.

Though his question was like a dagger through her heart, she said steadily, 'Yes.'

'What you *expect* from the relationship when you choose to love someone?'

She shook her head. 'I don't think you *can* choose. It just happens. Attraction, magnetism, love—call it what you like, but you can't argue with it.'

'Give me your definition of love.'

'It isn't easy to explain.'

'Try.'

'Very well. I believe it's an emotion that touches both the heart and soul. A delight in the essence of another person. A *caring* that puts the loved one before self…'

'From your definition it's quite clear you didn't love *me*.'

When she just looked at him, he quoted, '*A caring that puts the loved one before self...* If you remember, I came a very poor second to your career.'

Watching the colour drain from her face, he went on, 'So, as I can't believe you ever loved me, your argument falls down. Things are no different this time from what they were then. Now, are you ready to take off your clothes?'

'No.'

'It would be a lot less humiliating than having me strip you.'

In an odd sort of way he was right. Even if she struggled, she couldn't win—and what would it do to her pride to be ignominiously stripped?

It would trample it into the dust.

Taking a deep, shuddering breath, she pulled off her loose silky top, and then, her fingers shaking so much they could hardly perform their task, unzipped her skirt and stepped out of it.

Standing in her undies, she hesitated, half hoping he would relent, but one swift glance at his face told her clearly that there was no chance of that.

Wielding the whip of determination, she took off her slip and her dainty bra and briefs. Then, standing naked, she lifted her chin and looked at him squarely. 'Satisfied?'

'Not yet. But I intend to be.'

His eyes travelled slowly over her with a studied insolence that made her face burn with shame.

'Beautiful as ever,' he commented. 'But too thin. You could use a few more pounds.'

'Gerald preferred me slim,' she said defensively.

'Did he ever see you naked?'

When she refused to answer, David drew his own conclusions. 'No, I rather thought not. If he had, things might have been different. A man kept at arm's length can only handle so much mental foreplay without cracking. Whereas I, knowing I'm soon going to be able to sate myself, would like you to stretch out on the bed, like some beautiful butterfly, so I can feast my eyes on you and anticipate all the pleasure to come.'

Though at one time she had gloried in the fact that he found her beautiful, now she flinched away from the thought of being so *exposed* to his gaze.

'But first…'

Uncrossing his ankles, he rose leisurely to his feet and strolled over to her.

With a tremendous effort of will she managed to stand her ground.

He took each of her rosy nipples between a finger and thumb and pinched them gently, smiling a little when they firmed to his touch.

'That's better. Now you look—'

All at once overwhelmed by a feeling of total humiliation, and unable to stand any more, she covered her face with her hands and burst into tears.

His arms went around her, and with one hand cradling her head against his chest, his mouth muffled against her hair, he begged, 'Don't cry. I know I've been an absolute swine to you, but please don't cry.'

He sounded like the old David, and his obvious concern at how far he'd pushed her was balm to her wounded spirit.

But, having now given way, she was unable to regain control, and found herself trembling like a leaf and sobbing helplessly.

There was a sweetness to him, a gentleness completely at odds with his earlier deliberate cruelty, as, murmuring incoherent little words of comfort, he rubbed his hand up and down her spine.

When she continued to sob he picked her up and carried

her over to the bed. Putting her down, he stripped off his robe and slid in beside her. Then, pulling the light duvet over them both, he drew her back into his arms.

Despite spending the afternoon in bed, worn out emotionally, she was asleep again within moments, an occasional catch in her breath making her sound like a child who had cried itself into exhaustion.

His face tender, concerned, he cradled her while she slept.

She was dreaming. Dreaming that David was holding her, that they were back in those halcyon days when they had loved each other and the world was a wonderful place.

He held her tenderly, his chin resting on her hair. She could hear his heartbeat beneath her cheek, feel the movement of his chest as he breathed. The *rightness* of it brought its usual glow of happiness, and, sighing, she snuggled closer.

His arms tightened protectively.

Stretching out a hand, she stroked his jaw, her fingertips following the cleft in his chin before moving up to his lips. When he kissed the slim fingers that were tracing his mouth, eyes closed, she raised her face invitingly.

He kissed her lightly, sweetly.

She opened her mouth and he deepened the kiss. Her breathing quickening and a tingling warmth spreading through her, she rubbed one smooth, silky leg against the roughness of his.

In response, he stroked her gently, almost reverently—her arms, her shoulders, her neck, her ribcage, her slender waist—as if every part of her was precious, every part important to him.

Her breasts ached for his touch, and when his hand finally found their firm softness her pulse began to do funny things and she kept forgetting to breathe.

Though her entire being responded to his slow, skilful

caresses, she said nothing. Because there was nothing to say that his hands didn't already know.

Still in a dreamlike state, she began to caress him back. There wasn't a part of him that she didn't love, that didn't give her pleasure—his muscular chest, with its small, leathery nipples, his lean waist, his taut belly…

She heard his indrawn breath, then his fingers closed lightly round her wrist and he whispered softly, 'You'd better stop. Unless you *want* me to make love to you…?'

'Mmm,' she murmured, and, wriggling her wrist free, caressed his firm flesh once more.

He eased her onto her back, and a moment later she felt his weight with a surge of gladness.

They fitted together as naturally as if they were two halves of a whole, and her body responded joyfully to his long slow thrusts with an urgency that catapulted them both skywards.

Even when that first urgency was satisfied, their lovemaking was explosive, ecstatic. It seemed so long since they had made love that, awake or dreaming, like someone who was starving, she couldn't get enough of him.

When she awoke, late-morning sunshine was pouring in, filling the room with light and warmth. Her mind was alive with images, but she knew instinctively, without turning her head, that she was alone in the big four-poster.

Had David slept beside her? Had they really made love? Or had it all been just a dream?

Though the whole thing still had a dreamlike quality, her body felt sleek and satisfied. She knew without a shadow of a doubt that it had been no dream. She also knew that *she*, not David, had instigated it.

Her love and need had undermined her.

Somehow, without intending to, she had let go her sense of outrage at his actions, past and present, abandoned her pride, betrayed her principles, debased herself in her own eyes as well as his.

And, while her thinking brain roundly condemned her weakness, she knew that she had passed the point of no return. Though he had feet of clay, she still loved him and was his for as long as he wanted her.

But, feeling as she did, it couldn't be a happy union. Always at the back of her mind would be the knowledge of her own weakness and his betrayal…

The door opened and David came in carrying a tray. Dressed in smart casuals, he was freshly shaved, his dark hair tamed into neatness.

'Good morning,' he said with a smile. 'Or should I say good afternoon?'

While she felt ashamed, and embarrassed, he looked and sounded younger, happier, like the David of old.

Setting the tray down on the bedside table, he leaned over and, brushing a tendril of blonde hair away from her cheek, kissed her. A light but lingering kiss that made her heart beat faster.

'You're the only woman I've ever known who can wake up looking fresh and beautiful.'

No doubt he'd said that self-same thing to Claire.

As though he sensed her unspoken withdrawal, a shadow fell across his face.

Levering herself upright, she trapped the duvet under her arms to hide her nakedness while he plumped the pillows into place behind her before settling the tray across her knees.

It was set for one, with freshly squeezed orange juice, fluffy scrambled eggs, crisp curls of bacon and button mushrooms.

Finding her voice, she said awkwardly, 'Thank you. It looks and smells delicious.'

'Although it's lunchtime rather than breakfast time,

there's toast and marmalade, and coffee to follow. Speaking of which, I'd better go and rescue the toast.'

Watching the door close behind him, she felt an odd pang. In the old days when he'd brought her breakfast in bed he'd always either joined her or sat on the edge of the bed and been fed—or filched—titbits, while they talked companionably.

Now, though she wouldn't have known what to say to him, she missed his presence.

By the time he returned with the toast and coffee she was almost finished. He removed her empty plate and filled her cup with coffee. Then, sitting down on the edge of the bed, he watched her butter a piece of toast and spread it with tangy marmalade.

Glancing up, she saw him looking and, obeying a sudden impulse, broke off a piece and offered it to him. Instead of taking it, he leaned forward a little and opened his mouth.

Her heart doing odd things, she fed it to him, and watched while he chewed and swallowed.

A little blob of marmalade had escaped, and, his eyes holding hers, he took her hand. Putting her finger in his mouth, he sucked.

Desire kicked low in her stomach.

Somehow she tore her gaze away and continued with her meal.

'Laura rang this morning. She seemed more than a little anxious…'

'About Paul?' Deborah asked quickly.

'No, about you, and about how Gerald had taken the news that you weren't going back to New York. She said she knew you would feel guilty about cancelling the wedding at such short notice, and was hoping he wasn't making things too difficult for you. I told her it had all been sorted out, and promised we'd go in to see them this afternoon.'

Still in a state of mental upheaval, the last thing Deborah

wanted was to have to face them all, but, unwilling to say so, she nodded.

'In the circumstances, I thought it might be as well if you wore this.'

Before she realised his intention he had taken her left hand and slipped a ring onto the third finger.

Her breath trapped in her throat, she stared down speechlessly at the rainbow opal she had thought never to see again. Predominantly greeny blue, it changed colour with the light and glowed with its own inner fire.

'You kept it?' she said stupidly. 'Why?'

His voice casual, he answered, 'It's a nice stone. It took a lot of finding, and I didn't feel like parting with it.'

More than a little deflated—had she hoped he would say he'd kept it because of *her*?—she murmured, 'Oh.'

'Now, while you shower and dress,' he continued briskly, 'I've a few odds and ends of business to tidy up, and then we can get off.'

Without further ado he rose and, picking up the tray, departed.

Staring down at the opal, she felt an acute sadness, a keen sense of all she'd lost.

David hadn't offered to kiss her, and though the ring was back on her finger it was there under false pretences. Instead of being a promise of love and marriage and children, it was just there to make everything appear right in the eyes of the family.

Blinking back tears, she climbed out of bed and went to shower.

Some twenty minutes later, dried, and dressed in a taupe linen suit and a matt silk shirt, she was pinning her hair up when the door opened and David walked in.

Clearly his mood had changed. Now he looked serious, almost sombre, totally different from that smiling man who had first greeted her.

'I'm afraid something urgent has cropped up,' he told her. 'It necessitates a business dinner in town, so it would make sense to stay at Thornton Court tonight rather than driving back. I have clothes and things there, but you'll need to pack an overnight case of some kind.'

'Very well.' She was already reaching for her flight bag.

'I've had a word with Mrs Benjamin. She was planning to visit her sister this afternoon, and take the dog so she could stay the night. I've told her to go ahead and we'll do our own thing. I hope that's all right with you?'

'Quite all right. I can easily get myself something to eat.'

At the door David turned to say, a shade drily, 'Incidentally, she was very pleased that you'd changed your mind about getting married and living in New York, and even more pleased to know that we're "back together again".'

When she was packed and ready, Deborah made her way downstairs to find he was waiting for her in the hall. Taking her bag, he escorted her out to the car and settled her into the front passenger seat.

'Would you like some music?' he asked, when they were underway.

'Please.' It would be something to fill the silence that hung over them like a cloud.

A moment or two later the passionate music of Rodrigo's *Concierto de Aranjuez* filled the car.

Deborah had always loved the guitar concerto, and now it matched her feelings, with its sadness and longing, its poignant sense of loss.

She wondered if David had chosen it purposely.

St Jude's was busy, but many of the staff smiled at David and greeted him by name as they made their way up to Paul's room.

The various tubes gone, he was propped up on pillows and looking as well as Deborah could have hoped for.

When she bent to kiss him he gripped her hand and said in a heartfelt voice, 'Thank God you and David are back together again. Mum's delighted, and Kathy's over the moon. No doubt she'll tell you so herself when she gets back. She's popped out to do a spot of shopping while Mum looks after Michael. Not that he takes much looking after. He's as good as gold…'

They chatted for a while, but when the talk turned to business Deborah left the two men together and went through to the living accommodation.

The baby was fast asleep in his pram, and Laura was sitting on the couch, glancing through a magazine.

Tossing the magazine aside, she stretched out her arms and gave her daughter a warm hug. 'I can't begin to tell you how happy I am! I've always felt that you and David were meant for each other.'

A catch in her voice, she went on, 'Oh, love, you'll never know how I've hoped and prayed things would come right between you. And you're wearing your ring again. That's wonderful…'

Her eyes suspiciously bright, she sniffed. Then patting the seat beside her, said, 'Come and sit down and tell me how it all happened.'

Wondering briefly what her mother's reaction would be if she told her the truth, Deborah sat down on the couch. Unsure what to say, she prevaricated. 'Didn't David tell you?'

'Only that he'd persuaded you not to go back to the States and that you were together again. He didn't say how he'd managed to make you change your mind.'

Laura was nothing if not shrewd, and, knowing she would have to make it sound convincing, Deborah answered as truthfully as possible. 'It was simple in the end. He said he still wanted me, and I…I realised I didn't really love Gerald enough to marry him, that I'd never stopped loving David.'

CHAPTER EIGHT

LAURA sighed. 'Thank the Lord you realised in time.' A shade anxiously, she added, 'But what about your career? You won't want to give it up?'

'It no longer seems important.'

'Oh, darling, are you sure?'

'Quite sure. In any case, when I told Gerald the wedding was off, he said, "If you do this to me you're finished as far as your career goes. I'll make sure you never again work in the fashion industry".'

'Oh, dear!'

'I can't say I altogether blame him. All the arrangements have been made, and now everything's cancelled at the last minute...'

'No, the poor man must have been terribly upset.' Laura had always been compassionate.

'He was shocked and hurt, of course,' Deborah said carefully. 'But I rather suspect it's his pride that will suffer most.'

'Well, I hope he soon gets over it. Even wounded pride can be pretty painful.' Then with a determined change of subject, 'What do you think of Rothlands? Are you pleased with what David's done with it?'

'Yes, it's beautiful.'

'But something's not right?' Laura hazarded.

'What makes you think that?'

'You look rather like someone who's been to a wedding and a funeral in the same day.' Her face serious, she asked, 'You *are* happy?'

'Of course.' Aware that her voice lacked conviction,

Deborah added quickly, 'It's just that everything's happened so fast… I don't seem to have caught up, somehow.'

Her eyes searching her daughter's face, Laura observed, 'You don't *look* particularly happy. Are you still worrying about cancelling the wedding?'

'No, not really.'

'Then what's wrong?'

In spite of all her efforts, Deborah's eyes filled with tears.

'Oh, love…' Laura gathered her offspring close, and asked—as she'd used to when Deborah was a child—'Do you want to talk about it?'

'No… Yes… Oh, Mum, it's all such a mess…'

'What's a mess?'

Taking a deep breath, Deborah drew away and admitted, 'Everything.'

'There! I knew you were letting this wedding business worry you. But there's no way you could or should have married Gerald feeling as you do. Just hold on to the thought that everything will sort itself out. The important thing is that you and David love each other and are back together again.'

'But that's just it,' Deborah cried. 'David may still *want* me, but he doesn't love me any more.'

'Of course he loves you. He was absolutely devastated when you gave him back his ring.'

'He might have loved me once, but now he's angry and bitter because he thinks I put my career first.'

'Well, love, you did,' Laura pointed out gently.

Deborah shook her head. 'I didn't.'

'You told us all that your career was more important than marriage.'

'That wasn't true. It was just an excuse to save my wretched pride.'

'I don't understand,' Laura said blankly. 'If it wasn't true, why did you break your engagement?'

'Because David and Claire were having an affair—'

'Having an affair? No! You must be mistaken. David loved you.'

'Perhaps he did, but it didn't stop him having a fling with Claire.'

Laura shook her head, as if to clear it. 'What makes you so sure he had a fling with Claire?'

'She admitted it.'

'Knowing her, she could easily have made the whole thing up. She was always jealous of you. If *she* wanted David and he wouldn't look at her… Surely you've heard of sour grapes?'

Her mother was saying very much what Paul had said three years earlier.

'If she couldn't get him,' Laura went on hardily, 'I wouldn't put it past her to try to wreck your happiness… And if you believed her tissue of lies, she almost succeeded.'

'There was more to it than that,' Deborah said, and, with her hands clasped tightly together, told her mother what she had seen that Christmas Eve three years ago.

'You're certain?' Laura demanded. 'You couldn't have made a mistake?'

'No, I'm quite certain.'

'Things aren't always what they seem. It could have been quite innocent on David's part.'

Deborah was sighing inwardly at her mother's eagerness to make excuses for David when Laura added urgently, 'I've just thought of something. He's a rich man—suppose she was trying to set him up?'

'How do you mean?'

'She must have been pregnant around that time.'

'The baby was David's,' Deborah admitted painfully. 'Claire told me so. Which means he'd been sleeping with her while he was engaged to me.'

'Nonsense!' Laura said hardily. 'If the baby had been David's he would have sorted things out—even if he hadn't wanted to marry the wretched girl. He wouldn't have abandoned her and the child.'

'No doubt he wanted to keep it a secret.'

'If he'd wanted to keep it a secret, surely it would have made more sense to pay her to keep her mouth shut? No, I don't believe a word of it. David isn't that kind of man. He has far too much integrity,' Laura insisted.

'He's a red-blooded male—'

'But he's not a philanderer. Why would he risk indulging in a hole-and-corner affair when he was about to marry the woman he loved?'

'Perhaps in a weak moment he—'

'If, in a weak moment, he did cheat on you, rather than being angry and bitter because you'd left him, wouldn't he be ashamed?'

'He once told me he was a one-woman man, but he's shown no trace of guilt or shame over fathering another woman's child.'

'Which makes me even more convinced that he's totally innocent,' Laura stated.

Shaken by her mother's absolute certainty in the face of so much damning evidence, Deborah wondered for the first time if she could have made a mistake.

But that was just wishful thinking.

Stubbornly, she repeated, 'I know what I saw on Christmas Eve. And afterwards Claire as good as told me the child was David's.'

Laura shook her head. 'As I keep saying, things aren't always what they seem. She could have been lying. Personally I've no doubt that she was. It's a great pity you didn't go straight to David, instead of trying to save your pride.'

'Perhaps it is... But it's much too late now to alter things.'

'I never thought you were a fool,' Laura exclaimed vexedly. 'It may be too late to change what's past, but you *can* change the present. Rather than let him go on believing that you put your career first, why don't you tell him *why* you left him, and ask him straight out if he had an affair with Claire? I don't believe for a moment that he'd lie. And at the very least it would help to clear the air...'

As she spoke the door opened, and David walked in.

'Everything all right?' Laura asked.

'Everything's fine. But Paul needed a rest, so I've left him in peace.'

As though picking up the emotional tension, he glanced from one woman to the other. 'Been having a heart-to-heart?'

Laura summoned up a smile. 'You could say that. Now, shall I get you both a nice cup of tea? Kathy should be back any minute.'

Deborah could have done with a cup of tea, but, feeling too tense to face her sister-in-law's pleasure that she and David were together again, she said, 'Not unless anyone else wants one.'

David shook his head. 'We'd best get off. I've a business appointment later this evening, so we're staying overnight at Thornton Court. Tell Kathy we're sorry to have missed her, but we'll pop in tomorrow morning before we start for home.'

Deborah gave her mother a quick hug, and in response to her searching look nodded, and said, 'I think you're right.'

Laura's relief was patent.

The walk back to the car and the late-afternoon journey to Lowry Square were accomplished in silence. David appeared to be concentrating on his driving, and Deborah was sunk deep in thought.

Though she was—or had been—convinced of his guilt, she was loath to hear him admit it. And if he denied it, how was she to believe him?

When they reached Thornton Court, she went through to the kitchen to put the kettle on while David carried her bag straight upstairs.

She wondered briefly if he intended to put it in her old room, or if he was expecting her to share his bed. But instead of dwelling on it, her mind went back almost immediately to her resolve to follow her mother's advice and clear the air.

When he returned, she was still trying to decide how best to broach the subject.

Sitting down in one of the rocking-chairs, his well-shaped head tilted a little to one side, he watched her make the tea, and get out the crockery and milk.

Glancing up, she met his blue gaze. Abruptly her thoughts scattered in all directions and her movements lost their smooth efficiency and became jerky, so that the cups rattled in the saucers and she spilt some milk whilst filling the jug.

Making an attempt to pull herself together, she poured the tea and, despite knowing that it hadn't stood long enough and was weaker than he liked it, handed him a cup.

Almost as if he knew what was going on in her head, he remarked, 'You seem *distraite*. Something bothering you? Regretting the loss of your career, perhaps?'

It was the opening she needed. 'No. My career doesn't matter any longer. It never really did.'

'Oh, come on! It was all-important.'

'When I first left college it *seemed* important.'

His voice smooth, yet abrasive as pumice stone, he said, 'It must have ''seemed'' important for the past three years.'

'It was all I had left after our engagement ended.'

'It was your choice to end it. Your career then, as now, was a great deal more important than me.'

'It isn't now. It never was,' she admitted.

'Forgive me if I doubt that.'

'When Delcy Fashion House first approached me I turned their offer down. Because it meant moving to Paris and I didn't want to leave you,' Deborah revealed.

His face like granite, he asked, 'So what made you change your mind?'

'When I found out what was going on, I just couldn't stay—' Her voice broke. 'I had to leave you. I only said it was because of my career to save my pride.'

'Perhaps you'd like to tell me exactly what you're accusing me of?'

Her throat full of shards of hot glass, she said, 'I'm accusing you of having an affair with Claire—of fathering her child.'

'At last!' he said, with almost savage triumph. 'Laura has managed to get you to say what I couldn't. Although I pushed you to the limit.'

'You mean you *knew* I knew?' she asked confusedly.

'I knew what you *thought*. Paul told me.'

'When?'

'The night he had his accident. I was with him in hospital when he regained consciousness for a short time. When he asked for you, I promised I'd get you. But then he mumbled something about not wanting to die until he'd told me the truth.'

'B-but if you *knew* why I left you, why were you so angry and bitter when you saw me again?' she stammered.

'I was angry and bitter because you believed everything Claire told you. Love should mean trust, and you didn't trust me enough to even *ask* me. You wrecked both our lives on no more than her say-so. Without giving me a chance to defend myself, without me even *knowing*.'

'It was more than Claire's say-so. I actually saw you together,' she accused.

He looked puzzled. 'You *saw* us together?'

Her hands clenched into fists, nails biting deep into her palms, and she said, 'Remember that last Christmas, when there was a house party here at Thornton? We'd agreed, for the sake of propriety, not to share a room...'

Laura tended to be a little old-fashioned, and they had been careful to respect her feelings.

'You and Claire had adjoining rooms...'

The guests having been given the larger, *en suite* bedrooms, Deborah had been happily occupying what had once been one of the servant's rooms.

'It was Christmas Eve, and very late...'

Wearing her night things, and carrying her towel and sponge bag, she had been returning from the bathroom, her feet squeaking a little on the polished floorboards, when she had seen Claire leave her room, clad only in a diaphanous nightie.

Rooted to the spot, Deborah had watched her friend creep along the corridor and, after a moment's hesitation, as though she was afraid of waking anyone, tap lightly on David's door.

'I saw you open the door, and the pair of you kiss passionately. A second later you disappeared from view and the door closed.'

'I see. Then what did you do?'

'I—I went back to my room.'

'And you believed the whole thing was planned?'

'What else could I believe?'

'Didn't it strike you as odd that if it was a planned assignation she should have *knocked*? If she'd known the door would be open and I'd be waiting for her, wouldn't she have just slipped inside?'

As Deborah thought about it, he added, 'No doubt she

tried to, but when I'm travelling on business I stay in a lot of hotels. Through force of habit the door was locked.'

Remembering the way Claire had paused, one hand on the knob, Deborah found herself believing him.

'The instant I opened the door, she threw herself into my arms and kissed me. When I heard the knock I thought it was you, so she took me by surprise.'

'That might be true, but as soon as she was inside you closed the door.'

'When I stepped back, under the momentum, *she* closed the door. If only you'd waited a few more seconds, instead of running, you would have seen her unceremoniously ejected,' he insisted.

Her mother had said, 'Things aren't always what they seem. It could have been quite innocent on David's part,' and for the first time, Deborah wondered if she could have totally misjudged what she'd seen.

Still the doubts lingered. 'I don't understand why Claire should have gone to your room uninvited.'

'To achieve her own ends, no doubt.'

'Which were?'

'To break us up. She knew the sleeping arrangements—knew you'd be leaving your room to go to the bathroom before going to sleep. I wouldn't be surprised if it was all carefully staged. All she had to do was listen for you going and coming back, then make her move when she was sure you'd see her. She didn't know me all that well, so she might have thought there was a chance I'd be tempted. Even if I wasn't, so long as you'd seen her go into my room she'd achieved her aim. Even if you'd decided on a showdown, the evidence would have looked pretty damning. But, knowing what kind of woman you are, she probably guessed that you'd turn tail and run.'

It fitted together and could almost have been the truth. Almost.

Watching Deborah's face, he asked, 'Not convinced?'

'How can I be? I *know* you had an affair with her.'

'I did *not* have an affair with her!'

'Whether it was an affair or just a one-night stand makes little difference if you're the father of her child.'

'It was neither. And I'm not.'

'I wish I could believe that.'

'You can.'

Deborah shook her head. 'Claire said afterwards—' Breaking off, she cried passionately, 'Oh, what's the use of keeping on talking about it?'

'Go on—I'm interested. What *did* she say?'

'That you were the father. Oh, not in so many words. But there was no mistaking what she meant.'

'Tell me exactly what she said,' he insisted.

'She said, "Isn't it strange to think that if you have a baby our children will be related?" When I just gaped at her, she walked away—laughing.'

David got to his feet and, his face set and pale beneath its year-round tan, said with quiet emphasis, 'Once and for all, I am *not* the father of her child. I couldn't *possibly* be. Apart from that one kiss you witnessed, I haven't so much as touched her. She means nothing to me, and never has.'

Shaken by the ring of truth in his voice, Deborah stared at him, *wanting* to say goodbye to her doubts, wanting to believe him.

He looked back at her, his expression holding a kind of desperate resolve. 'To have the faintest chance of getting back what we once shared, you have to believe me unreservedly.'

A muscle jerking spasmodically in his jaw, he added huskily, 'If you can't trust me enough to do that, then we've no future together.'

His words, the anguish on his face, and the way she felt

about him, tore at her heart so that she couldn't speak. All she could do was wait for the worst of the pain to pass.

She stood in silence. As though fighting for self-control, he walked to the window, his arms hanging by his sides, his hands balled into fists, and stood gazing out.

Staring at his broad back and hearing again, 'I am *not* the father of her child. I couldn't *possibly* be,' she felt all her doubts disappear—washed away like sandy footprints at the ocean's edge.

If only she had talked things over with him, rather than believing Claire's lies, she wouldn't have cost them three precious years—wouldn't have lost his love and made him angry and bitter.

But it was no use fretting over what couldn't be changed. If there was the faintest chance of them getting back even part of the happiness and joy they had once shared, it would be worth fighting for.

Her heart thumping and her legs unsteady, she crossed to where he was standing.

'David…?'

When he remained still and silent, despite her appeal, she put her arms round his waist and rested her forehead against his back. 'I do believe you.'

His muscles tightened just for an instant, then he turned to look at her and she saw the love and longing in his eyes.

'I'm sorry…so sorry,' she whispered. 'From now on you'll have my complete trust.' Needing contact, she stretched out a hand towards him.

Taking it, he held it against his cheek.

The tenderness in the gesture made her want to cry. Instead, she smiled at him shakily.

He kissed the hand he was holding, before releasing it and drawing her close.

Her whole being overflowing with relief and thankfulness, she melted against him while he kissed her cheeks, her temples, her closed eyelids, and finally her lips.

When she put her arms round his neck, his hands came up to frame her face, and she heard his heart thudding as hard as hers. But he made no move to take things any further, and after a moment or two she drew away.

When he stood, quietly waiting, she realised that rather than rushing her he was allowing her to distance herself, giving her the option, the time and space he thought she might need.

But keeping her distance was the last thing on her mind. Reaching for his hand, she led him out of the kitchen and up the stairs.

When they reached the landing, she hesitated.

Smiling, he said softly, 'My room.'

She would always remember the sensations she felt as he undressed her: the shivers that shook her when he stroked her naked flesh; the pleasure that filled her when he kissed her; the desire that burnt her up when he caressed her breasts.

Then finally, when he'd stripped off his own clothes, the heat of his body was against hers. The sound of their breathing quickened as they began to move as one.

Their coming together was blissful, ecstatic.

After all the trauma of the last few days there were no words to describe how wonderful it was just to love and know herself loved in return. It made their lovemaking more than just a physical act—put it on a higher plane than mere sex.

Afterwards he cradled her in his arms and kissed her tenderly. He still didn't tell her he loved her, but he didn't need to. She had seen it in his face and was satisfied.

She had fallen into a kind of sweet languor when he said reluctantly, 'I'd like to stay just where I am, but my appointment's for seven-thirty, so I ought to be moving.'

The reminder was like a dash of cold water. Not wanting him to leave her, she suggested, 'You couldn't postpone it? After all, it *is* Saturday.'

He drew away with a sigh. 'I'm afraid not. It's something important that has to be dealt with as soon as possible.'

Watching him get out of bed and head for the bathroom, Deborah found him beautiful beyond words.

Everything about him made her heart leap. The set of his dark head and the way his hair tried to curl into his nape; the broad shoulders that tapered to a trim waist and lean hips; the firm buttocks and long straight legs.

But his physical appearance was only part of it. What lay beneath the surface made him the man he was, and had always been of prime importance.

There was something about him that pierced her heart and answered some basic need. He was her other half, a perfect match she might have searched the universe for and not found.

Yet somehow she *had*. Only to almost lose him through her own lack of faith.

But now they had found each other again, and this time, with boundless love and trust, they would have the rest of their lives together.

It was so long since she had been really happy that she wanted to pinch herself to make sure she wasn't dreaming…

When he returned, bringing with him the cool freshness of aftershave and the faint, masculine scent of shower gel, she was still lying back on the pillows in a contented, trancelike state, visualising their future.

'Planning to wait there for me?' he asked, as he started to pull on his clothes.

'Certainly not.' She tried to sound brisk. 'When I've showered, I shall probably cook myself a meal.'

He leaned over to kiss her, and, aroused afresh by the

lingering passion of his kiss, she only just stopped herself asking him to hurry back.

Once again answering her unspoken thought, he said, 'I'll try not to be too late.'

Somehow—maybe because everything had happened so fast—she needed the reassurance of his presence, and as soon as the door had closed behind him she felt a ridiculous sense of loss and panic. She wanted to run after him and beg him not to go.

But she was just being foolish. It wasn't as though he'd walked out of her life for ever. There might still be some difficulties ahead, but they were together now, and would stay that way.

This sudden change of mood simply meant that at the moment she was over-sensitive. Perhaps, after so much emotional turmoil, it was only to be expected.

Partially reassured, she climbed out of bed, found her toilet things, and went to shower.

Ten minutes later, dried and dressed, she made her way downstairs. Not particularly hungry, and no fan of television, she found herself a book to read while she waited for David to come back.

Gilding the Lily failed to hold her interest, and, unable to totally shake off the strange mood that had clouded her new-found happiness, she felt both forlorn and restless.

Suppose she went out for a walk? It had to be better than just sitting here all evening waiting, and if she passed a likely looking restaurant she might even stop for a bite to eat.

Collecting her jacket and shoulder-bag, she closed the door behind her. The evening was still relatively mild, though the sky had turned cloudy.

Her mind on David, and all that had happened, she had left Lowry Square and was wending her way along

Lightham Street when a familiar voice cried, 'Well, hello there!'

'Ben! How nice to see you.'

Ben Winnet had been Paul's best friend since their school-days. Short and plump, cuddly and amiable as a teddy bear, he'd always been one of the family's favourite people.

'Long time no see,' he said wistfully.

'I've been in the States for over three years.'

'Yes, I heard you'd become a very successful designer and were living in New York. I presume you're home because of Paul's accident? What's the latest news?'

'Though he's still fairly weak, he's off the critical list.'

'Thank the Lord!'

'Mum and Kathy and the baby have been staying at the hospital to be near him.'

'Yes, I know. Benjie, bless her heart, has been keeping me in the picture. By the way, is Paul up to having visitors yet?' Ben enquired.

'I don't see why not.'

'If you think it would be OK, I'd like to pop in to see him.'

Deborah smiled. 'I'm sure it would. But you could always check with Kathy first.'

'Thanks, I'll do that. Are you going to the hospital now?' Ben asked.

'No, we—David and I—were there this afternoon.'

'You're staying at Thornton Court?'

'Just for the night.'

'Has David gone back to Rothlands?'

'No, he has a business dinner in town.'

'So where are you off to?'

'Nowhere in particular. I just felt a bit restless, so I was taking a walk.'

When he seemed disposed to linger, she asked, 'What about you?'

'I had a special evening consultation.'

Deborah knew that, despite his innocuous appearance, he was a brilliant psychoanalyst.

'Now I'm off to get a meal. Have you eaten yet?'

'No, I haven't,' she admitted.

His smile diffident, he suggested, 'I suppose you wouldn't care to join me?'

Welcoming the distraction of his company, she agreed, 'Thanks—I'd love to.'

He beamed at her. 'This is my lucky night. Will Jerome's suit you? Though the food is unpretentious, it's always first class…'

Jerome's was a select, split-level restaurant just off Lightham Street South. David had taken her there on more than one occasion in the past, and it had always been well-patronised.

'Will we be able to get in on a Saturday night?'

'It's where I usually eat, so they know me there,' Ben said modestly.

'Then it'll suit me fine.'

'Great! Let's go.' Falling into step beside her, he remarked tentatively, 'When I last saw Kathy she told me that you were getting married quite soon, to your American boss.'

'I was. In fact it should have been today. But things didn't work out…'

'Oh… I—I'm terribly sorry. I hope I haven't…' He floundered to a stop.

'That's quite all right,' she reassured him. 'I realised that if I married Gerald I'd be making a terrible mistake.'

'Still carrying a torch for David?'

Ben knew all about carrying torches. Though he'd been

aware from the start that it was hopeless, he had loved Deborah since she was sixteen.

'You could say that.'

'I never did understand why you two split up… So, are you together again?'

'Yes.' Suddenly *believing* it, she smiled, her heart-shaped face radiant.

Selflessly warmed by her happiness, he said, 'I'm pleased.' Then, showing he missed very little, 'I wouldn't have mentioned it, only I saw you were wearing your opal.'

'Yes,' she said simply. 'Luckily David kept it.'

'It's beautiful and out of the ordinary. Exactly right for you.'

'It was David's choice.'

'I fancy the majority of men would go for diamonds, and the majority of women would be only too pleased.'

'Gerald's ring was a diamond cluster, but I much prefer the opal,' Deborah admitted.

'I don't blame you. So, you won't be going back to the States?'

She shook her head. 'I'm home to stay.'

'That *is* good news. I know the family will be only too pleased to have you back. They've missed you something rotten. Your mother in particular. The last time I saw her she…'

He was still talking cheerfully when they reached their destination.

As soon as they were inside the elegant foyer the *maître d'* came to greet them. 'Good evening, sir, madam. Your usual table, sir?'

'Please, André.'

The place appeared to be comfortably busy as they were escorted through the bar and seated at a window table on the upper level.

When the *maître d'* had finished reciting the chef's speciality dishes, Ben turned to Deborah and asked, 'What do you fancy?'

'As you know the menu, perhaps you'll order for me?' she suggested, and watched his fair face flush with pleasure at the implied compliment.

The order given, André summoned the wine waiter with a glance.

While Ben studied the wine list, Deborah looked around her. Though it was well over three years since she had been to Jerome's, apart from a few minor changes to the décor it appeared to be unaltered.

There were perhaps a dozen tables in all, six on each level, with the two levels screened from each other by a vine-covered trellis that helped to bestow a feeling of intimacy.

'I think a Château Frederic,' Ben decided.

'An excellent choice, if I may say so,' the wine waiter agreed.

Looking pleased that his taste in wine had been praised in front of the woman of his dreams, Ben waxed lyrical. 'A decent white Bordeaux is hard to beat. When I was in France last summer…'

While they sipped a cool, dry sherry, he launched into an interesting and exhaustive discussion on French vineyards.

At length, afraid he might be boring her, he said, 'But enough of that. It's time you told me all about your plans for the future.'

CHAPTER NINE

WITH so much still unsettled, there were no plans to tell him about. 'We haven't made any at the moment,' Deborah admitted. 'Everything's happened so quickly that it's all in the air. Which reminds me… The last time I saw you, all your plans were in the air too. You were trying to sell your flat and buy a house, so you'd have space for your model railway.'

'After months of frustration I managed to get rid of the flat. Then I bought a house in Vidal Street, where there's loads of space and an attic big enough to lay out all the track…'

Once he was riding his pet hobby-horse, someone to listen and ask the odd intelligent question was all that was necessary to keep the conversation flowing.

Well-entertained, and with food every bit as good as she recalled, Deborah found the time passed quickly.

They had finished their coffee before Ben, who was obviously on a high, asked hopefully, 'Do you need to get back? Or would you like to go on somewhere?'

'I really ought to get back. If David arrives home first he'll wonder where I've got to.'

'Of course.' Trying to hide his disappointment, Ben waved for the bill.

Seeing he looked crestfallen, and genuinely sorry to disappoint him, she added, 'I can't thank you enough for a lovely evening. I've enjoyed every minute of it.'

'It's been my pleasure.'

The bill paid, and a hand at her waist, he escorted her down the steps. They were skirting the lower level when

Deborah's glance was drawn to a table in the far corner of the room where two people, a man and a woman, were seated, deep in conversation.

David she could have picked out of a million men. And, although she hadn't seen the woman for over three years, there was no mistaking Claire's lovely profile and flaming red hair.

She was leaning towards David, her scarlet-tipped hand resting on his dark sleeve, a seductive smile on her face.

Ben, looking in the opposite direction, hadn't noticed them, and, feeling as though a red-hot stake had been driven through her heart, somehow Deborah kept putting one foot in front of the other.

When they reached the street they found it was just starting to spit with rain. 'Shall I get a cab?' Ben asked solicitously.

'No, it's not far. I'll walk.' Her voice sounded strained in her own ears.

Apparently noticing nothing amiss, he offered gallantly, 'If you like, I'll walk with you.'

Needing desperately to be alone, it was the last thing she wanted. But anxious, even in her stricken state, not to hurt his feelings, she tried to soften the blow. 'Better not. You live in the opposite direction, and if it does come on to rain fast you'll get wet.'

'That doesn't matter in the slightest—' he began. Then, picking up her tautness, 'You think David might not like another man seeing you home…?'

When she didn't immediately answer he said quickly, 'Don't worry. I quite understand. In his place I'd feel just the same… Well, give him my regards.' With feeling, he added, 'I hope he knows what a very lucky man he is.'

Ben's last words echoing hollowly in her ears, she began to walk blindly, neither knowing nor caring where she went, but needing to keep moving—as though by walking hard and fast enough she could outstrip the pain.

Her brain felt jarred, incapable of coherent thought. All she could see in her mind's eye were those two heads, one dark and one bright, so close to each other.

The rain—heavy now, and persistent, soaking through her thin jacket and drenching her hair—brought her back to some kind of awareness.

Still she walked. But bleak and bitter thoughts full of desolation and despair began to churn through her mind.

If she hadn't met Ben and gone to Jerome's she would never have suspected a thing. When David had said 'a business dinner' she had believed him implicitly. She hadn't for a moment suspected that he might still be seeing Claire.

Though this time round David had never said he loved her, she had believed he did, and for a short time had been happy. Now all that happiness had flown, leaving her more miserable and disillusioned than ever. The whole structure of her life in ruins.

She almost wished that she had stayed at home and simply waited for him. Then she would have been spared all this pain.

But what was the point of living in a fool's paradise? Better to face the truth, even if it hurt.

And the truth was that David's assertion that there had never been anything between Claire and himself, that her child wasn't his, was just a tissue of lies. His *You have to believe me unreservedly* was just a cynical con.

Obviously there had been, and still was, a great deal between them.

But if he had Claire, why did he want *her*? Why had he pressured her into cancelling the wedding and staying on? Was he taking some kind of revenge because, unwilling to play second fiddle to another woman, she had left him?

Another thought struck her. If, for the past three years,

David *had* been carrying on an affair with Claire, how had he managed to keep it from the family?

Laura knew Claire had left her husband and gone to live with another man, but apparently she had never suspected that man might be David.

Though if it *was* David why hadn't Claire taken their son? Why weren't the pair of them installed at Rothlands, rather then herself?

It made no sense.

But neither did the alternative. If it *wasn't* David, and Claire preferred another man, why were they still seeing each other?

Unconscious of the strange looks she was getting from the few pedestrians who were still about, she kept walking aimlessly while she went over the whole thing again and again. Finding no answers. Making no sense. But unable to let it go.

A blow to her shoulder spun her round and brought her to an abrupt halt. Realising that she had walked into a man coming in the opposite direction who, head down, was holding an umbrella, she began to stammer an apology.

Cutting her off with an impatient gesture, he was about to walk on when, noticing her white face and saturated state, he asked, 'Are you all right?'

'Yes… Yes, of course…' Seeing he looked unconvinced, she added quickly, 'It's just that I couldn't find a cab.'

'It's amazing how they all disappear in this kind of weather,' he agreed, sounding more human. 'Have you far to go?'

'No, I'm almost home,' she lied.

'Well, good night.'

'Good night.'

The little encounter had focused her, and, standing shivering, she wondered what to do for the best. She couldn't walk round London all night. Apart from anything else, it wouldn't be safe.

Perhaps she could book into a hotel?

But at this time of night, soaked to the skin and with no luggage, she wouldn't have the nerve to try. And what was the point of running away? She would have to face up to things sooner or later.

Turning in the direction of Lowry Square, she forced legs that suddenly felt like cold, wet indiarubber to carry her.

By the time she reached the house she was frozen to the marrow and completely exhausted. As she stumbled up the steps the front door was thrown open and David appeared.

In the light from the lantern she saw that he was still fully dressed. His hair was dishevelled, as if he'd been running distracted hands through it, and his face looked pale and strained.

He drew her inside, and, his usual calmness gone, burst out, 'Where the devil have you been? If you were going out why didn't you leave a note? I've been half out of my mind with worry. I was practically on the point of phoning the police and checking the hospitals in case you'd been involved in an accident… Dear God, look at the state you're in! You're icy cold and soaked to the skin. It'll be a miracle if you're not suffering from hypothermia. Let's get you straight into a hot bath.'

He urged her towards the stairs and, finding her legs would hardly support her, lifted her into his arms and carried her as easily as if she were a baby.

Once in the bathroom, he set her carefully on her feet and, one arm around her waist, turned on the bath taps and poured in bath foam.

As the bath filled and fragrant steam rose he stripped off her sodden clothes and tossed them into the dirty linen basket.

Far too numb to make any protest, she stood shivering

and swaying slightly while he removed her watch and took the pins from her hair, then checked the temperature of the water before helping her into the bath.

As she leaned her head against the headrest and let the blessed heat enfold her the shivers gradually died away and life came back into her deadened limbs.

Only her heart remained cold.

'Sit up a bit.' Reaching for the shampoo, he set about washing her hair. When he'd rinsed it, and rubbed it almost dry, he asked, 'All right if I leave you for a minute?'

She nodded.

By the time he returned, her nightdress over his arm, she was half-asleep and the water was cooling rapidly.

Having pulled the plug, he helped her out and dried her swiftly and efficiently on a soft white towel. There was no suggestion of the lover, nothing remotely erotic or sensual about his actions. His manner was that of a parent with a child, or a nurse with a patient.

Slipping the nightdress over her head, he said, 'Straight to bed now.'

When she opened her mouth to say she didn't want to spend the night in his bed, he cut her off short.

'It's quite obvious you're out on your feet. Explanations can wait until the morning.'

Too tired to argue, she climbed into bed and, leaning back against the pillows, struggled to keep her eyes open while she sipped the hot chocolate that was waiting on the bedside table.

Almost before the mug was empty she was fast asleep. David took it from her hand and eased her into a more comfortable position. Then, stripping off his own clothes, he got in beside her. Gathering her to him, he kept her warm with his own body heat.

When she awoke it was morning. A grey, leaden morning that matched her mood. Glancing at the bedside clock, she saw it was nearly a quarter to ten. She was alone, and glad to be. She needed time to think, to decide what she was going to do.

Should she face David with what she'd seen? Watch him squirm?

She didn't want to.

Still, in her heart, she wanted him to be the man of integrity she'd first thought him. She didn't want to hear him admit to being a cheat and a liar, see him for what he really was.

But what other option had she got?

None.

Apart from the fact that he would want some explanation for the state she'd arrived back in last night, she couldn't bear to stay with him and pretend nothing was wrong…

The latch clicked and David came in, carrying a tray of tea and biscuits. Shaved and dressed, his dark hair parted on the left and neatly brushed, he looked his usual calm, controlled self.

Remembering his almost wild appearance of the night before, she felt her heart contract with a feeling that might almost have been pity. He'd looked as if he *cared.* Yet how could he? If he loved *her*, why was he still seeing Claire?

Was it possible to love two women at the same time?

Why not? Guinevere had loved two men. King Arthur with her head and Lancelot with her heart. Perhaps David had been caught in the same kind of trap…?

His blue eyes studying her face, he asked, 'How are you feeling this morning?'

Empty. Desolate. Gutted.

Pushing herself into a sitting position, her ash-blonde hair falling in a silken tangle around her shoulders, she said, 'Fine.'

'You don't look it.'

He put the tray down on the bedside table.

In a detached sort of way she noticed it was set with the best rose-patterned china that Benjie kept for special occasions.

'Mrs Benjamin, who hurried back from her sister's to get our breakfast, wondered where you'd got to. I told her you'd had a late night. Heaving a romantic sigh, she said she quite understood…'

It struck Deborah that he seemed to be talking for the sake of it while he weighed up the situation.

'She was all for bringing up a breakfast tray,' he went on. 'But I persuaded her that tea was probably what you'd like. Of course if you're hungry…?'

'I'm not.' She had never felt less like eating.

When he'd poured the tea, and added just the right amount of milk, he sat on the edge of the bed and watched her drink it, his eyes brilliant between thick, dark lashes.

Though she knew him for what he was, his closeness still had a devastating effect on her, and she had to try hard to appear unmoved.

When her cup was empty he took it from her and put it back on the tray.

Then, as though suddenly restless, he got to his feet and walked over to the window. His back to the room, he stood looking out to where a pale, watery sun was breaking through the clouds and gilding the trees in Lowry Park.

After a moment or two he turned and said evenly, 'Now, would you like to tell me what happened last night to make you end up in that state?'

She took a deep breath. 'I discovered that you'd been lying to me when you said Claire meant nothing to you.'

His handsome face betraying no emotion, he suggested, 'Perhaps you wouldn't mind explaining how you "discovered" that?'

'I—I went for a walk, and met Ben Winnet. He asked me to have dinner with him...'

Though it was quite obvious now that he knew where this was leading, he ordered, 'Go on.'

'He took me to Jerome's.'

'And?'

Her voice leashed, under control, she said, 'I saw you there with Claire.'

'I see.' His eyes narrowed a little. 'Why didn't you come over?'

'We were on our way out.'

'So once again you jumped to conclusions and ran. Where's the belief? The trust you promised me?'

'How *can* I believe you? How *can* I trust you? You said you had a business dinner.'

'It *was* business.'

'If you expect me to believe that—'

'I *do* expect you to believe it. It happens to be the truth.'

Tightly she asked, 'What kind of *business* could you possibly have with Claire?'

'She told me that neither the man she's currently living with nor her estranged husband will have her son. She wants to make some long-term provision for the boy's future. At present he's being taken care of by her married sister who, with three children of her own, can't keep him indefinitely.'

'So she came to you?'

'That's right.'

'And you want me to believe that you *haven't* been seeing her? That you're *not* the child's father!'

'I haven't, and I'm not.'

'Then why did she come to you?'

'Because I have money.'

'Why should she expect you to support a child that's not yours? You must take me for a fool,' she cried bitterly.

At that instant there was a knock at the door, and the

housekeeper's voice called, 'Mr David? There's a Mrs Hopkins on the phone.'

'Thanks, Mrs Benjamin. I'll be right down.'

He gave Deborah a quick glance and opened his mouth as if to say something. Then, apparently changing his mind, went without a word.

As soon as he'd gone Deborah jumped out of bed and pulled a change of clothing from her overnight bag. Desperate to get away, she dressed as quickly as possible and repacked her few belongings, before dragging a brush through her tangled hair with so much force it made tears spring to her eyes.

She was pinning it into place when she realised she was still wearing the opal. Leaving the ring on the bedside table, she gathered up her overnight bag and her shoulder-bag, and, hurrying along to the landing, peered into the hall.

To her great relief it was empty. David must be using the phone in the living-room, as she'd hoped.

If she could slip out while he was occupied she could book into a hotel until she had had time to think, to decide what to do for the best.

She crept silently down the stairs and crossed the hall. Her hand was on the front door latch when his voice, querying softly, 'Going somewhere?' made her jump out of her skin.

Spinning round, she found he was much too close for comfort.

Taking her left hand, he added, 'And without your ring.'

'You'll find it on the bedside table. I've had enough of your lies and deceit. I'm leaving.'

When she attempted to open the door, his fingers closed around her wrist. 'I think not.'

'You said yourself that if I couldn't trust you we had no future together.'

'I also said that I wanted you. That hasn't changed. So I'm afraid I can't allow you to leave. A bargain's a bargain.'

'Even though I was forced into it?'

'If you were so desperate not to be you could have tried calling my bluff.'

'So it *was* bluff!'

'Of course,' he said coolly.

'What would you have done if it hadn't worked?'

His smile was mocking. 'Found some other way to make you stay.'

The thought of sharing him with Claire was anathema to her. Green eyes flashing, she rounded on him. 'Now I know you're still seeing Claire *nothing* would make me stay! I wouldn't be part of a harem three years ago, and I won't now.'

'I'm not asking you to. I'm asking you to believe that Claire means nothing to me and never has. I'm asking you to take my word that our meeting last night was purely business.'

'I *can't*. I'm going.'

Sardonically, he asked, 'What will the family think if you walk out on me a second time?'

Refusing to be pushed any further, even for the sake of family unity, she cried, 'At the moment they all think you're Mr Wonderful. So if you don't want them to know just what you're capable of, you'd better let me go now.'

He shook his head.

'In that case I'll tell Paul and the others the whole sorry story.'

'Very well.' He opened the door. 'Let's go.'

When she hesitated at the top of the steps, biting her lip, he asked tauntingly, 'What's wrong? Changed your mind about telling them?'

'No, I haven't. And as soon as I've told them the truth

I'm going to book into a hotel. I never want to set eyes on you again.'

Knowing she would have given her soul to have things differently, she went blindly down the steps into a morning that was becoming bright and warm.

He followed her, and, taking charge of her luggage, opened the car door.

She got in, careful not to look at him, and fastened her seatbelt.

Throughout the silent journey—already regretting her stand, but aware that she'd gone too far to back down—she stared fixedly out of the window.

When they reached the hospital, they found that, to add to the Sunday morning air of piety, a church service was being relayed to the wards. The opening hymn, 'All Things Bright and Beautiful', was being sung as they made their way up to Paul's suite.

Laura greeted them warmly, then said, 'Paul's still having his midmorning nap, and I'm afraid you've just missed Kathy. She's taken the baby out for a breath of fresh air. I hope you're not in a hurry?'

'Not at all,' David answered.

'Well, now you *are* here, I'd like to take the opportunity to go to the service in the chapel, if you don't mind?'

'Of course not,' he assured her.

Turning to her daughter, she asked, 'Would you like to come with me? Or would you prefer to stay and talk to Paul?'

David's blue eyes met and held Deborah's, a challenge in them.

She picked up the gauntlet. 'I'll stay and talk to Paul. You go ahead.'

Turning to Laura, David offered, 'I'll come down with

you. Let Deborah have a few minutes alone with her brother.'

When the pair had gone, Deborah went quietly through to Paul's room to find he was just stirring.

On seeing her, he raised a smile. 'Hi, sis… All on your ownsome? Where are the others?'

Deborah told him, then asked, 'How are you feeling this morning?'

'Fine.'

Though he answered immediately, something told her he wasn't speaking the truth.

Seeing she looked unconvinced, he added sturdily, 'I'm feeling better every day…'

She could believe he was—physically. But, knowing him so well, she felt sure there was something on his mind—something worrying him.

'I'll be up and about before too long,' he added for good measure.

'Don't forget you've been at death's door, so don't try to rush things.'

He grinned briefly. 'You've been taking nagging lessons from Mum and Kathy.'

Though his grin was a shadow of its former self, she was pleased to see it.

'So, how are things with you and David?'

It was obvious that he was expecting a favourable answer. She hesitated.

His eyes on her face, he remarked, 'You don't look terribly happy.'

'I'm not,' she admitted.

'Is it to do with cancelling the wedding?'

She shook her head.

'Why don't you come and sit down and tell me what *is* bugging you?'

Once she was settled in a chair by the bed, he pressed, 'Well?'

She half shook her head. Now it came to the crunch she couldn't do it. All the family thought the world of David, and she couldn't risk destroying their faith in him, the warmth and affection that now existed between them.

'Forget the clam act,' he told her. 'Get it off your chest. I don't like to see you looking so depressed. What's wrong?'

Knowing it was no use prevaricating, she admitted, 'It's all over between David and me. I'm leaving.'

Paul looked stunned. '*All over…* Why?'

'Things just aren't working… That's all.'

'You don't expect me to buy that, do you? Come on, sis,' he urged. 'There must be a *reason*.'

'He's still seeing Claire,' she said flatly.

'He's doing nothing of the kind—'

'It's no use,' she broke in. 'I saw them together with my own eyes. Last night, while he was supposed to be having what he called a ''business dinner'', I went for a walk. I happened to meet Ben, and he invited me to eat with him. He took me to Jerome's. David and Claire were there.'

Paul muttered something half under his breath that sounded like, 'Oh, hell!'

'I ought to have faced them there and then, but I couldn't. I was too shattered…'

'What *did* you do?' Paul asked heavily.

Her voice was unsteady as she told him, 'I walked about for a long time in the rain, then I went back to Thornton Court. This morning I told David what I'd seen, and asked him what kind of business he could possibly have with Claire. He said that the man she's living with has refused to keep her son, and so has her husband, and she wanted to make some provision for the boy's future. Previously he swore that the child wasn't his, and at first I believed him. But why should she go to *him* if he isn't the father? Why should she expect any man to support a child that's nothing to do with him?'

Then, in despair, 'I can't stay with a man who lies to me, who's involved with another woman—'

'David isn't involved with Claire.'

'It's no use trying to defend him. He's Claire's lover and—'

'Listen to me, sis! It's high time you knew the truth. David isn't and never has been Claire's lover. *I* was. *I'm* the father of her child. When he agreed to meet her last night it was on *my* behalf.'

Deborah felt as if she'd been kicked in the solar plexus. *Isn't it strange to think that if you have a baby our children will be related?* Claire's words seemed to be branded on her brain.

Because of what she'd seen that Christmas Eve, and the way Claire's words had been phrased, she had linked them with marrying David and having his child. She had never for a moment connected them with Paul. But now they made perfect sense.

She was filled with relief that she'd been wrong about David—that he hadn't lied to her, that he wasn't involved with Claire. Then she saw the look of desolation on Paul's fair face and her heart went out to him.

'I've made such a mess of things,' he muttered hoarsely. 'Not only am I responsible for everything that ails the company, but I've almost ruined your life and David's.'

There was such abject misery in his voice that she instinctively reached for his hand as he went on.

'When you first told me why you'd ended your engagement I was staggered. I knew Claire had always fancied David, and when you said you'd seen them together I wondered for a minute if he *could* be involved with her as well. Then, knowing David, I felt sure you must have made a mistake, jumped to the wrong conclusion… I wanted to tell you then about my part in it. But I was scared stiff that if I told a soul, if I once *admitted* it, somehow Kathy might find out.

'You'll never know how I blame myself for not coming clean. But when you said David meant less than nothing to you, I *wanted* to believe it. Kathy meant everything to me, and I was terrified of losing her… I took my happiness at the expense of yours and David's. And, though I could see how desperately unhappy he was after you left, God forgive me, I still kept quiet. All his kindness, all the help he gave me, was like coals of fire…

'When I had the accident I knew I had to get it off my conscience. I wanted to tell you together, but I was afraid I might die before you got there, so I told David everything. He listened very quietly, then he said, "Don't worry any more about it. I might well have done the same in your place." But I knew he wouldn't have—David's as straight as a die and the best friend any man could ever have.

'But when I asked him not to say anything I meant to Mum and Kathy. I thought he'd tell *you*, and when you two got together again, I believed he had. Otherwise I would have told you myself.'

Deborah felt as if her heart was breaking. David had known the truth for over a week, and though his own happiness had been at stake he'd said nothing.

'I only hope *you* can forgive me now you know that I'm the cause of all your misery.'

'Of course I forgive you. And you didn't cause it all. I'm as much to blame. If I'd trusted David more, even enough just to ask him for an explanation, things might have been different.'

'I hope knowing the truth will make you think again about leaving. You love David, don't you?'

'Yes.' It was just a whisper.

'Well, he loves you.'

'I wish I could believe that.'

'Come on, sis… He's always loved you.'

'I may have killed that love. He was hurt and bitter that I hadn't trusted him, that I'd jumped to the wrong conclusions. Now I've made that same mistake again. But seeing them together like that—it looked so *damning*. I just couldn't believe it was business…'

'Trying to deal with blackmail *could* be termed business,' Paul said bleakly.

'Blackmail?'

'That's what it amounts to. Or you might call it paying for old sins.'

'I don't understand how you got involved with her.'

'Unfortunately it was only too easy…'

The latch clicked. David was back. Glancing at the pair of them, he went to stand by the window.

Acknowledging his presence with a nod, Paul continued, 'Before Claire attempted to seduce David, she tried her charms on me, and I was naïve enough to fall for them. She was beautiful, sophisticated and alluring. And one night we ended up in bed together…'

He passed a hand over his face, plainly at the end of his strength, and said wearily, 'David knows what happened. He'll tell you the rest.'

His blue eyes compassionate, David took up the tale. 'When Paul met Kathy, he knew straight away that she was the woman he'd been waiting for. But, though Claire had said their affair was "nothing serious, just for laughs" she didn't want to let go. The harder he tried to let her down lightly, the more she clung. In the end he told her point-blank that he was in love with another woman.

'She wasn't pleased at being "thrown aside", as she put it, and Paul was scared stiff she would try and make mischief. When she turned her sights on Rory McInnes he was very relieved. But that relief didn't last long. A few weeks later she turned up at his office and insisted on seeing him. She told him she was expecting his baby—'

His face pale and strained, Paul broke in, 'The times fitted. And though I'd been careful to take precautions nothing's foolproof. She swore it could only be mine. When she saw how rattled I was,' he added hoarsely, 'she laughed and said, "Don't worry, I'm not asking you to marry me. And I won't even tell your tame little girlfriend so long as you provide enough money to keep me and the baby…" That's how the blackmail started.'

With a kind of shudder, Paul closed his eyes.

CHAPTER TEN

AFTER a moment or two David asked, 'Would you like us to leave?'

'No,' Paul said urgently. 'I want the whole thing out in the open. I want Deborah to know everything. Will you go on?'

David took up the story again. 'Things were already tight financially, but, as it was his responsibility, Paul promised that he'd find the necessary money. Instead of coming to me, he sold a block of the company's shares. Though they realised a reasonable amount of money, it wasn't long before Claire was asking for more.

'By that time she was married to Rory McInnes. She told Paul that her husband had known from the start that the baby wasn't his, but as he liked children he was quite willing to keep it—so long as it didn't become a financial burden. She promised that if Paul gave her a lump sum to invest for the child's future she would stay out of his life and never ask him for anything else. In order to find enough money to make that kind of investment he was forced to mortgage Thornton Court.'

Paul made a sound between a sigh and a groan. 'And it's all been for nothing. If Kathy ever found out—'

'She doesn't know?' Deborah breathed.

He shook his head. 'I was too afraid of losing her to tell her. And the longer I went on living a lie, the harder it was to admit what an idiot I'd been. I kept hoping that with the baby's future taken care of, and Claire safely married, I could put the whole thing behind me.'

Rubbing a hand over his eyes, he added bleakly, 'I should have known better.'

Seeing the despair on his face, Deborah's heart bled for him.

When he'd gathered himself, Paul went on. 'Just when I was starting to relax, Claire came back. She told me the company she'd invested in had gone bust and she needed more money. It was my own fault,' he admitted with some bitterness. 'I should have invested the money myself, rather than leaving it to her, but I was afraid of getting too involved in case anyone found out. When I told her there *was* no more money, she said, "Darling, don't be silly. You've a brother-in-law who cares about his little sister and who's worth a tidy few million. I'm sure he'd pay to keep her from learning the unsavoury truth."'

'I refused point-blank to involve David, but she threatened that if I didn't raise at least five thousand in double-quick time, she'd tell Kathy. I was wondering how on earth I was going to find five thousand when I took that bend too fast and crashed the car. Realising she wasn't going to get the money from me, she phoned David and said she wanted to see him "on business". When he turned her down flat, she suggested that he spoke to me.

'I'd told him everything, and he agreed to meet her for my sake. The trouble is, she knows perfectly well he's rich. And no matter how much he gives her she'll keep coming back for more...'

'There's only one way to put a stop to it,' Deborah said, 'and that's to tell Kathy yourself.'

'God knows I want to. But I'm frightened to death that if I do she'll take Michael and leave me.'

Remembering Kathy's face when they'd heard the news that Paul was off the critical list, Deborah told him firmly, 'Kathy won't leave you. After all, it isn't as though you cheated on her. It happened before the pair of you fell in love…'

'What happened before we fell in love?' Kathy's voice asked.

Neither Paul nor Deborah had heard the door open, and they both jumped.

Kathy came over and, having given her brother, her sister-in-law and her husband a kiss on the cheek, sank down on the bed.

'If it's something serious enough to make me think of leaving you, you'd better tell me quickly, before your son wakes up and starts yelling for his feed.'

Feeling hollow inside, Deborah got to her feet.

'Don't go, sis,' Paul said urgently.

With a worried glance at Kathy, Deborah hesitated. 'I don't really think it's my place to—'

'You and David obviously know what all this is about, so please stay, the pair of you.'

'If you're sure?' David asked quietly.

'Positive.' Turning to Paul and studying his wan face, Kathy observed, 'You're looking absolutely shattered. Perhaps you'd like to have a rest first?'

'No. I'd sooner get it over with…'

The latch clicked and Laura came in. 'Here I am—halo gleaming and chock-full of righteousness—' Becoming aware of the tension in the air, she broke off abruptly.

Her glance moving from David to Deborah, who was hovering uncertainly by the bed, then to her son and daughter-in-law, she asked, 'What's the matter? Is anything wrong?'

'I was just about to tell Kathy something I should have told her a long time ago,' Paul said.

'Sorry I just barged in,' Laura apologised. 'I didn't realise…'

As she turned to the door, Paul said quickly, 'No, don't

go, Mum. Come and sit down. I want you to hear it as well. Deborah and David already know.'

As Laura sat down carefully in a chair by the bed, helplessly drawn, Deborah went to stand by David's side.

Though there was a good foot of space between them, she felt the *frisson* of excitement that being near him always engendered. She had dared to hope that he might reach out an arm and draw her closer, but he made no move.

Glancing sideways, she met his eyes—and saw the bleakness in them. Her heart sank like a stone.

As they all waited in strained silence, Paul ran his tongue over his dry lips, and then, looking at his wife, began baldly, 'When I first met you I was having an affair with Claire Bolton. After a while she found she was pregnant...'

Head bent, staring down at the counterpane, Kathy sat still and silent while he poured out the whole sad tale.

'I should have told you. But I thought if you knew you might not marry me. And then, when we *were* married, I was terrified that if you found out you'd leave me... I've been an utter fool...'

Turning to his mother, he added, 'I've practically ruined the company Dad left, and brought it to the verge of bankruptcy. It couldn't be worse.'

'Yes, it could,' Laura disagreed. 'Money isn't everything. Only a little while ago we didn't know whether you were going to live or die. You may have been weak and foolish, but Claire's to blame for a lot of the harm that's been done.'

Hearing him sigh, she patted his hand. 'You must have been through hell. I just wish you'd told us sooner, rather than carrying a burden like that all on your own.'

'If it hadn't been for Deborah I don't know how much longer I'd have kept trying to hide it. But with David being involved...'

Seeing the look of surprise on his mother's face, Paul explained. 'Finding she can't get any more money out of me, Claire's trying to get her claws into David. And the Lord knows I've already done him and Deborah enough harm…'

'Knowing them both, I'm sure they've forgiven you—as I have,' Laura told him.

His worried eyes on his wife's face, Paul asked hesitantly, 'Kathy?'

For what seemed an age she didn't answer, then looking up, she said, 'Of course I forgive you. I only wish you'd told me straight away. It would have saved so much unhappiness.'

'I'm sorry I didn't. But I wasn't sure you cared enough. I should have had more faith in your love…'

That struck a chord, and Deborah glanced involuntarily at David. But his dark, attractive face was devoid of expression.

Kathy lifted her chin. 'Mum mentioned that Claire had left her husband and gone to live with another man… What's happened to the little boy?'

'Sean,' Paul filled in. 'At present he's living in Shepherd's Bush, with Claire's married sister. But she and her husband already have three children of their own, and I gather they're not very well off.'

'Perhaps a regular monthly payment directly to them…?' Laura suggested.

'Certainly in the short term,' David agreed. 'But I think it would be best if I provide a lump sum to make the child's future secure—'

'But Paul said that kind of thing has already been tried, and has failed,' Laura broke in anxiously.

'Unfortunately he handed over the money to Claire.'

'What did she do with it?'

'Last night I pressed her to answer that question. Finally she admitted she'd given it to her husband, who'd invested in a motorcycle maintenance business which had gone bust within eighteen months.'

Turning to Paul, he went on, 'This time I was thinking of setting up a fund, to be administered by trustees so that neither Claire nor anyone else can touch a penny of it.'

Paul gave a sigh of relief. 'If you're willing to do it, that sounds like a good idea.'

Quietly, Kathy said, 'I've got a better one…'

They all looked at her.

'The only way to make absolutely sure that Sean will be loved and looked after properly would be for us to adopt him.'

His voice hoarse, Paul asked, 'You'd really agree to that?'

'If he's your son,' she said simply.

'Oh, sweetheart,' he whispered brokenly, reaching for her hand. 'I've been worried to death about what might happen to him if Claire's sister didn't want to keep him.'

Kathy bent to put her cheek against his. 'Then stop worrying. Everything's going to be all right. I'm sure Michael will love to have a big brother. Now, you get an hour or two's rest while we start the ball rolling.'

As the four of them returned to the suite David put a hand on the small of Deborah's back. It was the kind of light, innocuous touch that he might have used to shepherd Kathy or Laura, or just any casual acquaintance, but it burnt through her suit and into her back like a brand.

When they were assembled in the living room, Kathy turned to her brother and asked, 'Where do you think we should start?'

He answered unhesitatingly. 'As Claire is only using the child for her own ends, I suggest we start with Mrs Hopkins.'

'Who's Mrs Hopkins?'

'Claire's sister. Though I had no intention of allowing Claire to blackmail me, I was concerned about the boy's welfare, so I decided to check things out for myself. I rang Mrs Hopkins first thing this morning and left a message. She phoned back and made me an appointment for this afternoon.'

'So you're going to see her?'

'Straight after lunch. Do you want me to sound her out about adoption?'

'Please.' Glancing from him to Deborah, Kathy asked, 'Would the pair of you like to stay and eat here?'

'No, I'll get off, thanks,' David refused. 'But Deborah might want to stay.'

She shook her head. 'I think I'll go with you.'

Giving them both an impulsive hug, Kathy exclaimed, 'I can't tell you how delighted I am that you two are together again! Thank the Lord all this mess hasn't totally ruined your happiness…' Then, a shade anxiously, 'Let me know how you get on with Mrs Hopkins.'

'Will do,' David agreed.

They kissed Laura, and, their goodbyes said, set off to walk back to the car park in warm sunshine.

Glancing at David, Deborah saw he was looking straight ahead, his face uncommunicative.

She sighed.

Her lack of trust had almost wrecked their relationship for a second time. But now all the cards were on the table surely the damage wouldn't prove to be irreparable?

Though his love had taken a hammering, he had refused to let her go, and while he still wanted her there was hope.

When they reached the car, David abruptly shattered that hope by asking coolly, 'Where would you like me to drop you? The nearest hotel, perhaps?'

A silken noose tightening around her throat, she shook her head.

'Thornton Court?'

'No, I…' She dragged air into her lungs. 'I'd like to go back to Rothlands with you.'

He lifted a dark brow in mock surprise. 'It's not very long since you told me you never wanted to see me again.'

'That was when I thought—' She broke off, biting her lip. 'I'm sorry…'

He looked at her, his face hard. 'If you do come back, it will have to be on my terms.'

'You mean I should be there and available whenever you want me?'

'That's exactly what I mean. If you have a problem with that—'

'I don't.'

'So how long will you give it this time?'

'I'll stay as long as you want me to.'

'Then what?'

'Find a job of some kind. Start again.'

'When I've finally got you out of my system you can always go crawling back to Delcy, make it worth his while to give you back your job.'

She flinched at his deliberate cruelty, then, collecting herself, said steadily, 'I won't be doing that. Even if I wanted to, Gerald doesn't believe in forgive and forget either.'

'Oh, I *believe* in it.'

'But only if it's a first offence?'

'More than once could be considered a weakness. Now, if you're still coming with me…?'

'Yes, I am.'

Opening the car door, he said coolly, 'Then I suggest we go and get some lunch. Mrs Hopkins is expecting me at two thirty.'

Her spirits at rock-bottom, she climbed in and fastened her seatbelt. It looked as though repairing the damage wasn't going to be as easy as she'd hoped. In fact it might prove to be impossible.

* * *

After eating a virtually silent lunch in a rooftop restaurant close to Hyde Park, they set off for Shepherd's Bush.

Mrs Hopkins lived at the far end of a pleasant row of terraced houses in West View, a quiet, tree-lined cul-de-sac. Drawing to a halt outside number twenty-eight, David helped Deborah from the car and, his manner cool and impersonal, escorted her to the front door.

His knock was answered almost immediately by a woman in her late twenties, wearing blue jeans and a white T-shirt. She was plump and pretty, with a cheerful face and an underlying air of contentment. Her red hair was taken up into a spiky knot.

'Mrs Hopkins?' David enquired courteously.

'Yes…?'

Deborah's first thought was that though Mrs Hopkins shared her sister's colouring, she was nothing at all like Claire.

'You must be Mr Westlake.'

'That's right,' he said pleasantly. 'And this is my fiancée, Miss Hartley.'

Deborah was jolted—until she realised he was merely explaining her presence.

'Won't you come in?' Mrs Hopkins said.

They followed her along a passage and into a sitting room that overlooked a small back garden, with colourful borders and a neat lawn.

Two children, a girl of three or four with red-gold hair and a dark-haired younger boy, were playing on the swings. In the next door garden an elderly woman was pegging out washing.

'Please sit down.'

When they were seated on a linen-covered settee, she asked, 'Can I get you a cup of tea or anything?'

'No, thanks,' David answered. 'We had a late lunch.'

Sitting down opposite, she weighed them up with blue eyes that were just a shade wary. 'You said you'd like to see me about Sean? What exactly is it you want?'

'I understand he's your sister's child, and that he's with you because neither her husband nor the man she has gone to live with want him?'

Her mouth tightening, Mrs Hopkins said, 'That's what it amounts to.' With a sigh, she added, 'Claire's always been selfish and flighty, but I don't know how she could turn her back on her own flesh and blood without a moment's concern or regret.'

David leaned forward a little. 'May I ask a very personal question?'

'Go ahead. Though I may not answer it.'

They eyed each other with mutual respect before he asked, 'Does she support the child?'

'No. Jos and I do. She told me that she'd been hoping to get the child's father to support him, but she'd had no joy.'

'You have children of your own—it must be a strain on your finances?'

'We manage,' she answered briefly.

'When I talked to your sister last night she mentioned that she was concerned because you might not want to keep him indefinitely.'

'She knows perfectly well that we're more than happy to keep him. He likes it here, and the poor little mite's better off with us. At least we *care* about him.'

A trifle bitterly, she added, 'Since he's been here she's never once visited him, so don't let her kid you she's a doting mother…'

At that moment the door burst open, and the little girl ran in, closely followed by the boy.

'Mum, Mum!' she cried, 'Mrs Dove says we can—' Seeing there were strangers present, she stopped in mid-sentence.

Mrs Hopkins put an arm around each of them. 'This is my daughter Katie, and this is her cousin Sean, who's come to live with us.' Then, to the children, 'Are you going to say hello to the lady and gentleman?'

'Hello,' Katie said immediately, while Sean looked at them with big brown eyes before shyly returning Deborah's smile.

Duty done, Katie turned to her mother. 'Mrs Dove says we can have some of her ice cream. Can we, Mum? Can we?'

'You both had a good lunch, so I expect so.' As the pair ran out, whooping, she called after them, 'Don't forget to say please and thank you!'

There was a chorus of, 'We won't,' before the back door slammed.

Smiling fondly, Mrs Hopkins said, 'Sorry about that. Mrs Dove likes to give them ice cream and biscuits, but I've told them to always ask me first.'

'The two of them seem to get on well together,' Deborah remarked.

'Apart from an odd squabble, they all do. Sean fits in very well. He's a lovely child—so good-natured and sunny. He's like the son we've always hoped for. Ours are all girls. We were planning to try again, but after my youngest was born there were problems and I was advised not to have any more. To tell you the truth, Jos and I would like to adopt Sean. It would give him some real stability. And I think Claire would be pleased to get him off her hands once and for all…'

Pulling herself up, she turned to David and said apologetically, 'I'm sorry. I'm rambling on, and I still don't know why you're here.'

'I wanted to talk to you about Sean's future, about making some financial provision for him.'

'Are you a lawyer?'

'No. I'm here in a purely private capacity.'

'You're Sean's father?'

'No.'

'But you know who his father is and you're here on his behalf?'

Expecting David to say yes, Deborah was surprised when he said decidedly, 'No. I have no idea who Sean's natural father is.'

'Then why are you willing to provide for him? What's your connection with my sister?' Mrs Hopkins wanted to know.

'Miss Hartley and she were at college together,' David answered smoothly.

'Of course!' Mrs Hopkins exclaimed. 'I couldn't think why the name Hartley was familiar...' Then, making the connection, 'So you're *David Westlake*.' She looked more than a little awed.

'Got it in one.' He smiled at her. 'That's why, when Claire was concerned about her son's future, she came to me.'

Proving she knew her sister well, Mrs Hopkins said, 'I don't want to sound unkind, but if you take my advice, Mr Westlake, rather than giving Claire the money you'll put it where neither she nor anyone else can get their hands on it.'

'That's what I intend to do. If you and your husband are in agreement, I thought perhaps a trust fund, that will keep Sean financially secure until he's eighteen? One which, whether you decide to go ahead and adopt him or just continue to take care of him, would provide enough day-to-day funding to take any financial burden off your shoulders.'

She sighed. 'That would be wonderful. Though we *could* manage without help, even if it just paid for his clothes and shoes, and things like that, it would save having to count every penny.'

'I think, for the good of the whole family, we can do considerably better than that.'

Sounding dazed, she said, 'I can't thank you enough. Both of you.'

He rose to his feet, and, like someone in a dream, Deborah followed suit.

As Mrs Hopkins escorted them to the door, he told her, 'When I've sorted out all the legalities I'll be in touch with you and your husband.'

'I can't thank you enough,' she repeated, and shook hands with them both.

The sky had turned cloudy, and as they stepped outside David remarked, 'It's just starting to spit with rain.'

'So it is,' Mrs Hopkins said. 'I'd better call the children in.'

Even so, she remained standing in the doorway until they had regained the car and driven off.

For a while they travelled without speaking. The only sound, apart from the purr of the engine, was the click of the wipers as a gusty wind threw handfuls of rain at the windscreen.

Needing to make contact, Deborah asked, 'Do you think they'll start adoption proceedings?'

'I hope so.'

'You don't foresee any problems?'

'There shouldn't be. They seem eminently suitable, and there's a blood tie.'

'Suppose Kathy and Paul are disappointed?' she ventured. 'After all, there's a blood tie there too.'

David shook his head. 'It's a pity Paul didn't ask for some proof that the child was his before he started paying out.'

'You mean DNA testing?'

'That wouldn't have been necessary. All he would have had to do was look at the child.'

'I admit Sean doesn't seem to take after him, but I don't see how he could be *sure*.'

David slanted her a glance. 'It's plain to see you did arts rather than science.'

'I don't know what you're—' She stopped abruptly. 'Of course! Both Claire and Paul have blue eyes—'

'As do I,' he pointed out drily. 'And it's genetically impossible for two blue-eyed people to produce a child with brown eyes.'

She felt almost giddy with relief. 'So Paul *can't* be Sean's father…'

'No.'

'I wonder who is.'

'Some one-night stand, I expect.' Contemptuously, he added, 'Claire probably doesn't know for sure, but she had to lay it at someone's door. No doubt Paul was the poor sucker who was the most gullible and had the most money.'

Deborah sighed. 'It's hard to believe that one woman could cause so much trouble and heartache… I just hope for Mr and Mrs Hopkins's sake that Sean takes after his father. It was incredibly generous of you to arrange a trust fund for Sean under the circumstances.'

When David made no further comment she relapsed into silence, her thoughts moving to an even more emotive problem. How to win back the love she had thrown away.

By the time they arrived at Rothlands the rain was pouring down. Drawing up as close to the door as possible, David helped her from the car and hurried her into the house.

Standing in the hall, uncertain, ill at ease, like a visitor unsure of her welcome, Deborah asked, 'Would you like me to make a pot of tea? I may as well earn my keep.'

He turned his cool blue gaze on her. 'If you're keen to "earn your keep" I can think of more enjoyable ways to do it.'

Seeing her flush, he added, 'However, a pot of tea will do for the moment. Perhaps you'd like to make one while I give Kathy and Paul the news?'

Deborah went through to the kitchen and put the kettle on. Then, feeling inwardly cold, and needing the comfort, she took some kindling and split logs from the basket and crouched to light the fire.

By the time David appeared a tray of tea was waiting on the low table in front of the fire and the logs were crackling and blazing cheerfully.

'A scene of cosy domesticity,' he commented, his voice sardonic.

Reaching to pour the tea, she asked, 'Do you have anything against cosy domesticity?'

'Not at all. Three years ago I was ready to settle for a lifetime of it.'

He crossed to where she was sitting and, producing a spotless hankie, tilted her chin and wiped a smear of soot from her cheek.

His touch unnerved her so much that when she handed him a cup she had a job to hold it steady.

For a while nothing was said, then, bracing herself, Deborah asked, 'How did they take it?'

'Naturally they were relieved. Paul cursed himself for being such a fool. But he's not the first to be taken for a ride by an unscrupulous woman, and I'm afraid he won't be the last. They were both pleased to know that, though the child isn't their responsibility, he's with a decent family and his future is being taken care of.'

He said no more, and they finished drinking their tea in silence.

Once upon a time silence between them had been comfortable, companionable.

Now it wasn't.

Fine wires of tension stretched between them, making

Deborah conscious of her own breathing, her own heartbeat, stretching her nerves to breaking point. There was so much to say, yet she seemed incapable of framing the words.

Glancing up, she saw he was watching her. His eyes were cool, waiting. It was obvious that he had no intention of helping her.

In desperation she went to kneel by his chair. Taking a deep, steadying breath, she said huskily, 'David, I'm sorry…so sorry… I don't wonder you're hurt and angry. I just wish I could make it up to you…'

'I'm sure you can. I was going to suggest an early night, but if you're eager to make a start…' He glanced at the thick sheepskin rug in front of the hearth, his little smile leaving her in no doubt as to his meaning.

'If that's *really* all you want from me…'

'You don't look too happy at the prospect?'

'I'm not.' She gave an involuntary shudder.

'If you hate my terms so much, why did you come back with me?'

'I had to try to make things right… I couldn't just walk away.'

He smiled mirthlessly. 'That's hardly the impression you gave me this morning.'

'Believe me, I'd give *anything* to take back what I said then—if only it were possible.'

Her eyes filled with tears, making them glisten like emeralds.

'You used to like *The Rubaiyat of Omar Khayyam*…'

She stared at him blankly for a second or two, not sure what he was getting at.

'If you remember, there's a certain passage in it that might answer your question.'

The passage he was referring to sprang to her mind, and without thinking she quoted. '"The moving finger writes; and, having writ, moves on; nor all thy piety nor wit shall lure it back to cancel half a line, nor all thy tears wash out a word of it.'''

'Exactly.'

'All right!' she cried. 'So what's done can't be undone. There's no going back. All I can do is ask for your forgiveness and go forward. You told me that if there was any future for us I had to trust you. I *wanted* that future. I *wanted* to trust you. But I...' The words tailed off as she struggled for control.

Gaining it, she went on, 'If *you* want that future you've got to at least *try* to see things from my point of view. I had no idea that Paul had been involved with Claire, and when I saw you and Claire looking so intimate together, after you'd said a *business* meeting, I was devastated... She had a hand on your arm and she was smiling at you as if she was offering herself...'

'She was—as part of the deal. It seems she never gives up. Needless to say, I refused her offer.'

'But I wasn't to know that... Oh, David, can't you see how it must have *looked*?'

His face still and shuttered, he said nothing.

She made one last attempt. 'But I've finally learnt my lesson. I promise I'll never doubt you again.'

With a shake of his head, he said flatly, 'I don't think you can promise that.'

Knowing she had failed, she felt a sense of utter despair. She had finally killed his love. All he felt for her was lust. All he wanted from her was what he'd said he wanted.

Rising to her feet, her eyes filled with bitter tears, she began to unbutton her blouse.

'Don't!' he said roughly.

Startled, she stammered, 'B-but I—I thought that was what you wanted.'

'It isn't.'

Reaching out a hand, he pulled her onto his knee. 'You

said you'd never doubt me again. And while I hope you won't ever have cause to, it's not something you should have to promise… On the two occasions you've seen Claire up to her tricks I've expected you to believe me. Because I knew I was innocent. I haven't been fair to you. I've expected too much. I should have realised how *damning* they both must have appeared. It's I who should be asking for forgiveness.'

Her heart taking wing, she suggested huskily, 'Suppose we agree to forgive each other?'

He drew her close and, his mouth muffled against her hair, said, 'But I want more than forgiveness. I want your love.'

'You have it.'

That earned her a kiss, before he went on, 'I want to go forward and leave what's happened behind us.'

'I want that too.'

When she was warm and glowing with his kisses, he pursued, 'I want you to marry me and stay with me for the rest of my life.'

With a sigh, she nestled against him. 'I think I can safely promise that—so long as you love me.'

'I've never stopped loving you.'

It was what she would have given her soul to hear, and her heart filled with gratitude and she lifted her face for his kiss.

After a while kissing wasn't enough, and she freed her lips to suggest demurely, 'Don't you think it's a shame to waste the opportunity?'

Blue eyes gleaming, he asked, 'What opportunity did you have in mind?'

'Well, the fire's just right, and that rug looks thick and comfortable, and Sarah's still away…'